"Hey, Let Me Up!"

Maggie wriggled and punched Mac's big shoulders.

"Feels great, doesn't it?" Mac levered himself up on his side, still pinning Maggie beneath the shallow current of Woodman Creek.

"Get off me." She tried to sound stern.

"Give me a single good reason why I should."

Maggie thought of several, but not one seemed to matter. For suddenly she felt an incredible lightness, as if she'd been carrying a huge weight on her back and someone—Mac, to be specific—had simply said, "Why don't you try putting that down?"

It was lovely, this lightness. It made it okay for her to do silly things like fall in Woodman Creek and then not get right back out again.

One of Mac's arms came behind her, supporting her. He brought her upright as he rocked back on his heels. Then he sat, lifting her neatly and settling her astride his lap. Maggie allowed all of this.

She wrapped her arms around Mac's neck. "I think—" she began.

"Yes?" he prompted.

"I think it's good to be alive.

Dear Reader:

Welcome to Silhouette Desire! If you're a regular reader, you already know you're in for a treat. If this is your first Silhouette Desire, I predict you'll be hooked on romance, because these are sensuous, emotional love stories written by and for today's women—women just like *you!*

A Silhouette Desire can have many different moods and tones: some are humorous, others dramatic. But they *all* have a heroine you can identify with. She's busy, smart, and occasionally downright frazzled! She's always got something keeping her on the go: family, sometimes kids, maybe a job and there's that darned car that keeps breaking down! And of course, she's got that extra complication—the sexy, interesting man she's just met....

Speaking of sexy men, don't miss May's *Man of the Month* title, *Sweet on Jessie,* by Jackie Merritt. This man is just wonderful. Also, look for *Just Say Yes,* another terrific romance from the pen of Dixie Browning. Rounding out May are books by Lass Small, Rita Rainville, Cait London and Christine Rimmer. It's a great lineup, and naturally I hope you read them all.

So, until next month, happy reading!

Lucia Macro
Senior Editor

CHRISTINE RIMMER

HARD LUCK LADY

SILHOUETTE *Desire*®

Published by Silhouette Books New York

America's Publisher of Contemporary Romance

SILHOUETTE BOOKS
300 East 42nd St., New York, N.Y. 10017

HARD LUCK LADY

ISBN: 0-373-05640-0

First Silhouette Books printing May 1991

Books by Christine Rimmer

Silhouette Desire

No Turning Back #418
Call it Fate #458
Temporary Temptress #602
Hard Luck Lady #640

Silhouette Special Edition

Double Dare #646

CHRISTINE RIMMER's

favorite pastimes include playing double-deck pinochle, driving long distances late at night, swimming in cold mountain rivers and eating anything with chocolate in it. She's also a voracious reader and an inveterate romantic daydreamer who's thrilled to have at last found a job that suits her perfectly: writing about the magical and exciting things that happen when two people fall in love. Christine lives in California with her young son, Jesse.

For my Granny, Sidney Francis Naisby Neall Strand,
who bequeathed to me a passion for words.

One

Maggie got out of the rental car. Once on her feet, she stretched out the kinks from all the hours of traveling by plane and by car. Then, when she felt she could no longer avoid it, she made herself look at the house.

The sight of it almost accomplished what the sight of her brother lying lifeless on a steel table hadn't been able to do; the sight of the house almost made Maggie Durrant cry.

Untrimmed lilac bushes obscured the side porch. Wild roses and rampant sweet peas twined the fence in front. What she could see of the building itself through all the overgrown bushes and vines didn't look good. The house was even shabbier—though that hardly seemed possible—than the last time Maggie had seen it, three years before. Reluctantly she approached and stood peering over the gate.

The white paint on the front pillars that supported the sagging porch roof was blistering and peeling off in strips.

The wood beneath the paint was the silvery gray that indicated dry rot. The front-porch floor had several boards missing. More than one pane in the three ancient double-hung front windows was cracked. The asphalt siding had cracked all over, too. The nubby gray outside walls now had a thousand black hairline fractures, like the veins on the back of an old man's hands.

"It's just a house," Maggie whispered to herself. "Just a house, that's all. We don't live here anymore, nobody lives here now." The threatening tears receded, and the lump in her throat went down. She felt antsy as a cat on a hot cast-iron griddle, but she was in control once more.

In an effort to relax a little, Maggie took a few deep breaths and let herself look everywhere but at the house she had to enter to find a decent suit of her brother's clothes.

To her left, across the street, the Conroy place looked much the same as she remembered, with its grape arbor gate and stone retaining wall. Nearer to where she stood, the cedars and Douglas firs that rimmed the clearing looked taller than she remembered. The birches and willows growing down to Woodman Creek behind the house seemed denser than they had been.

As her gaze wandered, she discovered something she'd never seen before. Across the creek, halfway up the hill, was a new house where the old Burkette place had once stood. At a glance Maggie had an impression of big windows and wood stained a natural color. Through the fanning branches of the trees, the late-afternoon sun created speckled patterns of light and shadow on the shingled roof.

A beautiful place, Maggie thought, one that fit gracefully into its surroundings. Judging by the big windows, it would be filled with light. She stared at the lovely new house for a time, finding its beauty soothing.

Then she turned back to the weathered gate in front of her, clutching the key that the funeral home had provided from her brother's effects and steeling herself for the task at hand. Maggie pushed the gate inward. Ancient hinges complained as she stepped into the yard.

The house had two porches. One at the front, with a door into the living room, and another along the side, with a door to the kitchen. Both were stacked with firewood and each had an old battered couch to sit on, along with a straight chair or two. When she was growing up, she had always used the kitchen door to go in and out. So, out of habit, Maggie mounted the side porch. At that moment a teasing breeze slid in from the back of the house and ruffled a piece of paper that was tacked to the kitchen door.

Puzzled, Maggie approached the door. It took her a few minutes to assimilate the information on the paper.

It was an eviction notice. It said that someone named MacEvan Manero was ordering Bryan Durrant to vacate the house within thirty days.

It made no sense at all to Maggie. After all, Bryan owned the house. Their mother had left it to him when she died. How could someone order him out of it?

Bewildered, Maggie went around to the front door. It displayed the same piece of paper. Numbly she pried the tack loose and took the paper in her hands.

She was so absorbed in staring disbelievingly at the notice that she hardly heard the squeaking of the gate. The deep, vibrant sound of a man's voice made her jump like a spooked rabbit.

"You must be Bryan's sister."

Maggie looked up from the notice and into a pair of eyes darker than her own. The man let the gate squeak closed behind him and came toward her.

He was a big man, taller than her own six feet. His features were broad and blunt, compelling in a rough-hewn, basic sort of way. He had the look of a Native American about him, in his high cheekbones and broad forehead. He smiled as he approached her. Maggie read the sympathy in those dark eyes immediately. Whoever this big man was, he knew that Bryan was dead.

But of course, she thought bitterly, everyone for fifty miles around will know by now. In her mind she could hear them all whispering:

Did you hear about Bryan Durrant? Got drunk and ran himself off the road at the North Fork Bridge down by Indian Glen. Now, I'm not one to speak ill of the dead, but that boy was a loser from the day he was born. Sad to say, blood will tell. Just like his father, too many big dreams and not enough plain sense....

The big man mounted the porch, his booted feet firm on the rickety boards. Maggie drew herself up, feeling immediately challenged by this man's very presence. He was too big, too imposing, too blatantly male—and his smile was too charming.

He boldly extended a hand. "Hello, I'm Mac Manero. I live across the creek." Maggie had a flashing vision of the beautiful, graceful house. This man must be the owner. "I saw you pull in," he said.

"Mac*Evan* Manero?" Maggie asked coldly, repeating the name on the paper she held.

"I prefer just plain Mac."

She couldn't make herself take the man's hand. She said, "I'm Maggie Durrant."

"Bryan's sister," he said again, as if seeking confirmation that his first assessment had been correct.

"That's right."

With the grace of a born diplomat, Mac Manero used the outstretched hand Maggie refused to shake to take the notice from her. "I apologize for this," he said ruefully, cocking a dark brow at the paper. "I should have thought to take the notices down. I realize they've probably just upset you more at an already difficult time."

Maggie sucked in a breath and tried her best to speak civilly. "Please explain the reason for them." Her voice sounded stilted, as if she were asking for directions in a language not her own.

The big man balled the notice in his fist. "It's beside the point now. Don't worry about it. Is there something I can help you with?"

"What do you mean, beside the point?" Maggie framed each word with studied care. She was on edge, and she knew she must, above all, hold on to reason. "This is my brother's house. What right do you have to kick him out of it?"

"Ms. Durrant—" Mac Manero began. His voice was infinitely kind and understanding.

Maggie cut in before he could really say anything. "Just tell me. Is this or is this not my brother's house?"

He drew in a breath. Then he said, "No, it's mine."

Maggie turned from him, from the kindness in his eyes and the sympathy in his voice. She stared at the ground beyond the porch, which was littered with rotting apples from the neglected Jonathan apple tree.

"Your brother sold me this house two years ago," Mac Manero went on. "He stayed on as a renter."

With an effort of will, Maggie turned back to face Mac Manero. She looked straight into his eyes. "And he hadn't been paying his rent," she said flatly of Bryan before the big man could say it first.

"I'm afraid that's about it," he said.

"And lately he hasn't been easy to pin down," she went on, her voice hard as quartz rock. "So you were forced to post the notice rather than give it to him in person."

Mac Manero looked uncomfortable. "Look, I'm sorry."

"Why?" she snapped, almost hating the man right then for being so kind, for pitying her and her brother. "It's not your fault that my brother never cared about paying his bills. It's just..." She sought the words and found none. So she finished bitterly, "That's just the way he was."

"I liked Bryan," Mac Manero said. "Everybody did. He'll be missed."

His kind words increased her defensiveness. She heard herself demanding, "How do you know who'll miss my brother? You're obviously new here. You don't know this town too well." She referred to the inhabitants of both Sluicer's Bar and the larger Brandy City a few miles away.

"He will be missed," Mac Manero said convincingly again, letting her hostility wash right over him and pass away unremarked.

Maggie felt ashamed. It wasn't this stranger's fault that Bryan hadn't honored his commitments. Nor was it his fault that Bryan had sold the family home and then gone two years without bothering to tell his sister what he'd done. Maggie knew very well that she was being unreasonably surly and mean. But her emotions were on overload and her guard was up.

With great difficulty she managed to murmur a thank-you for his kind words about Bryan.

"It's only the truth," Mac said.

Maggie looked at him. His hair, thick on top and neatly trimmed at the sides and back, was coarse and dark around his blunt features. His wide, full mouth still wore a hint of a smile. His obsidian eyes probed hers, as if he at once understood her pain and was willing to help her survive the crushing weight of it.

For a moment out of time, Maggie could almost see herself doing the impossible—laying her head against this stranger's broad chest, feeling strong hands stroking her hair, hearing whispered words of comfort and understanding.

But then she drew herself up short. She backed away from him a little, and her expensive linen skirt brushed against the end of the woodpile that was stacked beneath the windows. She knew the pile was dusty, and she was glad. It gave her an excuse to turn away from Mac Manero's overpowering gaze. She spent more time than it required to brush off her skirt.

When she was done, she explained, "I need some of Bryan's clothes to take back to the funeral home in Grass Valley."

"The funeral service will be there, then?" he asked.

"No, that's just where they took—" she swallowed "—the body. I stopped there on the way up to make the arrangements. The funeral will be in Brandy City. Day after tomorrow. I'll put up a notice at the post office."

"I understand," he said. Then he added a little awkwardly, "And of course you'll need to get in and out of the house to take care of things." He started to turn. "There's a spare key in the porch eaves, by the other door. I'll get it."

"No, it's all right." She stopped him, holding up the key in her hand. "They gave me the one from Bryan's things."

"Good," he said. She waited for him to murmur another sympathetic phrase or two and take his leave, but he just stood there.

She wondered if maybe he wanted to know how long it would take her to clear out the house. "I'll try to get everything out in a week at the most, if that's all right?" she asked.

"Yes. Of course. Take your time."

They went on looking at each other for a moment or two more, and Maggie was aware of the sound of the river some distance away. People in cities got used to the noise of cars going by, of sirens and of jets. Here in Sluicer's Bar, sister community to the county seat of Brandy City four miles away, it was the hollow murmur of the Yuba River that accompanied every moment of life. Maggie had always found the sound soothing and benign, but right now the endless distant roar seemed to mock her.

She said to MacEvan Manero, "I want to go in now. I'd rather be alone."

He was quiet, as if digesting what she'd said. Then he said, "No, I think I should stay."

Maggie felt her self-control slipping again. She struggled to hold on to it. "I don't understand. Are you afraid I'll steal something? That's ridiculous. Whatever's in there is my brother's, anyway."

His voice when he answered was very soothing. It set Maggie's teeth on edge. "I don't think it would be good for you to go in there alone right now. I think you're upset and could use a friend."

"No *man* tells me what's good for me." The words were out before Maggie could stop them. They were harsh, hostile words—words she might have thought but never would have uttered under less strained circumstances.

Mac Manero, however, refused to take offense. "Let me go in with you, Maggie."

"I want to be alone."

"Please," he said, his wide mouth curving upward again, "humor me."

Maggie stared at him. He was rare, in her experience. A man she couldn't get rid of. In general, she knew, she made men nervous. There was the sense about her that just maybe she was stronger than any man she could look level in the eye. And at six feet, Maggie Durrant stood equal with the majority of men. Mac Manero, however, was not only bigger than she was; he appeared to be every bit as strong willed.

"I'll be fine," she said grudgingly, hoping to get rid of him by reassuring him that she was all right.

"Okay." He reached for one of the dusty old straight-backed chairs that were bucked against the woodpile. He flipped the chair around and sat down, crossing one booted foot on a denim-clad knee. "I'll just stick around to see that you get what you need."

Maggie glared at him for a moment, irritated but no longer near to losing her self-control. Somehow, by refusing to take offense when she insulted him, he had diffused a great deal of her internal stress. And what could she do, after all? It *was* his house.

She shrugged. "Suit yourself."

He nodded. Maggie turned and stuck the key in the lock.

The old white-painted door swung inward, complaining louder than the front gate had done. Maggie stepped over the threshold.

Inside it was hot, cluttered and smelled of mildew, either from leaky pipes or perhaps rotting wood. She flipped the light switch to alleviate the dimness. It didn't work. Of course it wouldn't; if Bryan hadn't paid his rent, it stood to reason he'd have neglected the electricity bills, as well. Standing there with her hand on the switch, Maggie felt the floodlike force of a thousand memories assailing her at once.

She pushed them back by turning and marching resolutely to the downstairs bedroom, which was separated from the main living area by a dusty curtain printed with huge, twining roses. The bedroom had once been her parents' room, and then her mother's alone. It was logical to assume that Bryan would have claimed it after their mother's death three years ago.

Maggie's assumption was right. The room was a mess, the bed unmade. Bryan's clothes were everywhere. He'd never been one to pick up after himself, though in his personal hygiene he was quite clean and neat.

When they were children, and had each taken half of the long room upstairs, Maggie's end had always been immaculate, while Bryan's was a complete disaster area.

"Hey, Maggs, I can't help it," Bryan used to tell her with one of his most eloquent shrugs. "I'm a slob is what I am." And then he would smile.

Oh, how Bryan could smile. They used to joke between them that God gave Bryan "likability," and all He had left over to give Maggie was brains.

"And guts," Bryan used to add. "You got guts, Maggs. That's why you're gonna make it in life." Then he'd laugh. "And when you do, make sure you don't forget your baby brother...." Bryan had always called himself that: her baby brother. He was two years younger than she was.

Standing at the foot of the old brass bed, Maggie rubbed at her temples, willing the thoughts of Bryan away. Right now she couldn't afford to indulge thoughts of Bryan. She could do that later, after all of Bryan's affairs had been settled, after she had returned to the good life she'd made for herself in Arizona and had left the foothills of northern California behind for good. Now she needed to find the clothes quickly and get out of this house where the shadows were too thick and the memories too close.

She went to the closet, shoved back the curtain that screened it from the room and riffled through the things on hangers. At the back she found what she was looking for— a good gray suit still in plastic from the dry cleaner's. She looped it over her arm and marched back out to the porch.

Mac Manero stood up when she came through the door.

"Thank you." Maggie forced a smile for him. "I've found what I needed."

"Good," he said.

She turned, pulled the door closed and locked it, feeling overly conscious of the man who waited behind her. When she was done, she faced him once more.

"Where are you staying?" he asked.

"I'll take a room in town at one of the motels."

"If you need anything—" he began.

"Thank you," she said firmly. "But I don't need anything at all." She stepped around him then, smoothly, and picked her way over the missing boards in her high-heeled shoes.

Mac Manero watched her go, admiring the proud set to her shoulders and, more fundamentally, the slight sway of her hips beneath her skirt. Except for the marked physical resemblance—the dark hair and eyes, the tall, graceful body—it was hard to believe that the woman he'd just met was Bryan Durrant's sister. Bryan had been a soft charmer, content to while away his days, letting life happen to him.

This woman was as tough as flint. Integrity emanated from her like the steady beam of a lighthouse beacon. Judging by her clothes and the easy way she wore them, this woman had money and knew what to do with it. That, of course, fit with what Bryan had let drop about her over the past few years. Bryan had said his sister lived in Arizona, and that she was getting richer by the minute running a chain of video rental stores.

In the end, though, Mac didn't give a damn about whether Maggie Durrant had money or not. What intrigued him was her strength and the softness in her brown eyes, a softness he knew she hadn't wanted him to see.

She had lost a brother. Mac Manero knew what it was like to lose a brother. It was a pain you never really got over, but a pain that Mac had learned from. In a way everything that Mac was now could be traced back to its beginning in his older brother's death. Ritchie had died young and senselessly, and Mac had sworn he'd have more to show for himself when *his* time came.

Out in the sunbaked clearing, Maggie Durrant was getting into her car. Her thick, inky hair, which was rolled away from her face and pinned up at the back in a style reminiscent of the forties, showed glints of red in the light. She was behind the wheel and pulling away long before Mac was through looking at her.

She had said she'd post a notice about the funeral. Mac would be checking for that notice. It was a tribute, Mac supposed, to the immeasurable charm of Maggie's brother that Mac had never really felt angry with Bryan Durrant even when he fell over a year behind in rent.

That's Bryan, people in town always said. And Mac had come to understand exactly what they meant.

Mac was going to the funeral. Partly to pay his last respects to the memory of Bryan Durrant. But mostly to get another look into the secret softness in the depths of Maggie Durrant's cold eyes.

Two

The old white clapboard Methodist church on Mercantile Street in Brandy City was filled to overflowing. Those who'd come late stood at the back, since all the pews were full except the one in the front reserved for the family.

There Maggie sat alone wearing a black dress. Maggie kept her eyes straight ahead, on the masses of gladioli and hothouse lilies that she'd ordered for the service.

The fine mahogany casket beneath the altar was closed. Originally Maggie had thought to have it open, which was why she'd needed Bryan's good suit. But a day of deeper thought had convinced her that her brother was not his remains; let the mourners remember him vibrant with life.

As people got settled, the organist played pieces Maggie had chosen. Then the minister, a young man new to Brandy City, spoke briefly, sharing a few kind and well-chosen remarks about Bryan and his life.

Though the service was very short, to Maggie it seemed interminable. She could feel all the people behind her, crowding the pews, boring holes in her back with their eyes. She'd been prepared to be stared at; she had expected it. She'd wanted a fine funeral for Bryan—for the sake of his memory. Or at least, that's how she'd thought of it at first.

When her mother had died, three years ago, there had been no more than a brief blessing said at the gravesite. That was how Julie Foley Durrant had wanted it—*No fuss and nothing fancy,* as she'd written in her will. Maggie had respected her mother's wishes, but deep down she'd hated letting people think that she and Bryan couldn't afford to do the funeral up right.

The ugly truth was that she'd subconsciously wanted to rub the town's nose in her own success, to make them all see that at least one of those *Dreamin' Durrants* had done more in life than dream. With Bryan's death she'd had her chance to show them all. She'd jumped at that chance without thinking, in those first unreal hours after she'd learned Bryan was gone.

But as she firmed up the arrangements with the Grass Valley funeral home over the past two days, she'd begun to acknowledge the defiance in her gesture and to perceive that she had grown beyond the need to prove anything to the people here. By then, though, the whole process had been set in motion, and she'd decided to go ahead with it.

It was turning out to be a lot more difficult than she'd expected, not a triumph at all, to sit in the front pew alone and listen to the kind words of the young minister and realize that he was speaking about the brother she would never see again.

At least, Maggie reasoned bravely, she was holding on to her dignity. In fact, since those painful moments at the house she'd grown up in, her emotions had been in good control. Yesterday she'd concluded the funeral arrangements. She'd even found time for a stop at the courthouse to begin the process of having herself declared Bryan's administrator, since he had left no will.

"Let us pray," the minister said, bringing Maggie's thoughts back to the here and now. She bowed her head and let the soothing words wash over her.

After that it was time to proceed to the gravesite. One by one the rows behind her emptied out. For a few minutes Maggie was left alone in the old church in order that she might say her final goodbyes.

As yet, Maggie didn't feel it wise for her to dwell too much on thoughts of Bryan. Instead, she took those moments to sit quietly in the pew and to admire the simple beauty of the rough-hewn cross above the altar and the worn gold-leaf Bible that lay open there.

After a suitable time she rose and went out to the street, where a limousine waited to take her to the Sluicer's Bar cemetery four miles away.

At the gravesite Maggie sat beneath a canopy that had been erected for the burial. She found herself thinking that it was a beautiful day for her brother to come to his final resting place. Beyond the cemetery fence the wind blew the grasses on rolling fields that ended in the beginnings of tall forest. Closer, wild roses grew in profusion and California poppies peeked around weathered gravestones.

Her one friend from childhood, Allison Stanton—now Allison Clay—approached her before the interment began. Allison laid her cheek against Maggie's and said in her ear, "We're so sorry, Maggs. We all loved him, you know."

Maggie didn't reply, though she briefly squeezed her friend's shoulder to signal that the kind words were appreciated. Allison's kindness brought to mind MacEvan Manero the other day. He had been kind, too, when he told her that Bryan would be missed.

In retrospect Maggie was feeling a little contrite about her behavior with the big stranger. She'd been downright rude to him. She'd behaved just like the bitter adolescent who had left Brandy City fifteen years ago to make a new life for herself. Since then she'd learned to be civil with people, at least. A new start and eventual success had softened her hard edges a bit, taught her that a smile and a reasonable tone got a lot more done than a hostile demand ever could.

Allison whispered, "People didn't know where to bring things. Mac Manero suggested they open the old schoolhouse, and Netty Beach took it from there."

Netty Beach was a pillar of the local community, but Maggie wasn't thinking about her right then. The name that stuck in her mind was that of Mac Manero. Maggie sat up straighter. Had he been at the church—those dark eyes that saw too much staring at her back while she'd kept her own eyes studiously to the front?

Maggie forced a smile for her friend. "Bring things?" she asked, trying to collect her thoughts.

"You know, food and stuff."

"That isn't necessary," Maggie said quickly, wondering how she could have forgotten the rituals of life in a small community. When attending a funeral, one brought food for the bereaved family so they wouldn't have to bear the extra burden of preparing meals for a few days. "I mean, there's only me, and I don't really need it. I'm staying at the motel and I wouldn't be having to cook, anyway."

"Folks like to get together after," Allison said gently.

Maggie realized her friend was right. "Yes, of course. I didn't think."

"You'll come down to the schoolhouse, then?" Allison's voice was coaxing. "After this?"

Maggie's heart rebelled at the thought. She certainly didn't feel like eating anything right now. Besides that, she didn't know how she'd hold up having to stand around with a paper plate in her hand accepting condolences from all the people she'd detested when she was growing up.

But she just couldn't refuse. People were only being kind. She was an adult now, and wise enough not to turn her back on kindness.

"Of course I'll come," she said.

Allison gave her one more quick, reassuring hug and started to move away. Maggie realized almost too late that she felt very alone, all by herself in the row of folding chairs beneath the canopy.

Maggie whispered, somewhat urgently, "Stay, won't you? Sit here by me?"

Allison smiled that loving, open smile that had brightened at least one small corner of Maggie's shadowed childhood. "I was hoping you would ask," she said, dropping down in the next chair.

With her friend out of her line of vision, Maggie could see across to the knot of mourners that was forming on the other side of the grave.

One man stood heads above the rest, his coarse hair as black as ravens' wings. He wore a beautifully tailored double-breasted gray suit and looked as comfortable in it as he had in his boots and jeans two days before. He watched Maggie, his head tipped slightly to the side. He didn't smile. She felt that he was studying her and expressing compassion at the same time.

Once again, as she had on the steps of her family's ramshackle house, Maggie found herself drawn to MacEvan Manero. And, just as she had two days ago, she felt threatened by the attraction. Maggie forced herself to look away from his compelling dark gaze.

She glanced off toward the cemetery entrance—and recognized the one person she truly hated in all the world: her grandfather, Elijah Foley, former district judge of Del Oro County.

Leaning heavily on a dark wooden cane, he came through the cemetery gate. As he made his way up the steep slope that led from the gate to the place where his grandson would be buried, he kept his eyes straight ahead. Once or twice someone greeted him. He would nod without looking at the speaker, lofty as royalty, and pass on.

The bitter adolescent deep inside Maggie rose up. All the maturity and emotional balance she'd acquired in the fifteen years on her own fled as if they had never been. Maggie longed to do the unthinkable, to rise from her folding chair and order Elijah Foley to leave.

She wanted nothing from him, ever. He'd had the grace not to ruin the service for her with his unwanted presence; why couldn't he have stayed away from this last ritual, as well?

He was a cold, hard, old man who'd amputated Maggie and Bryan from his life before they were even born. When they were children, he used to turn and walk the other way if he saw them on the street. Elijah Foley was not and had never been a grandfather in any of the ways that mattered. His relationship to Bryan—and to Maggie—was an accident of blood, no more. Maggie had learned to accept that fact. And at that moment she hated the old man for his very presence, for being the living embodiment of all the rejections she'd known as a troubled little girl.

Quickly she turned away—and found herself looking right into the knowing eyes of MacEvan Manero. His expression was a probing one. Then he glanced down at the old man who was making slow, stately progress to the group around the open grave.

Mac looked back at Maggie. She hated him right then, almost as much as she did the old man for coming. But her animosity toward Mac Manero was for another reason altogether. His understanding glances invaded her privacy; her traitorous heart kept whispering, *trust him*.

Brandy City had a population of just over three hundred; Sluicer's Bar was home to ninety-nine souls. In communities that size, everybody knew everybody else's business. Mac Manero, though not a native, had clearly put down roots here—and he'd bought a house from Bryan and then become her brother's landlord. Of course he would know of the judge, and also of the bond of blood between Elijah Foley and the Durrants. What else he might know, Maggie didn't even want to imagine.

Mac moved then, edging his way out of the group. Maggie watched him, bewildered. Was he leaving? She resented his knowledge of her; she was unnerved at the way just looking at his blunt features tugged on her senses—but she didn't want him to *leave*.

Then she saw what he was actually doing. He approached her grandfather and offered the old man his arm.

Elijah Foley drew back at first and peered up at the taller, younger man disdainfully. Mac merely continued to hold out his arm, that charming smile of his warm and unwavering. Mac spoke to the judge, though Maggie couldn't hear the words. They were congenial words of greeting, she assumed.

Elijah Foley peered narrowly at Mac Manero for a moment more. And then he made a decision. He rested his arm on the younger man's and allowed himself to be helped the remainder of the way up the slope.

Maggie sat tall, refusing to look away as the two men came toward where she sat beneath the canopy. The wounded child within her cursed the funeral home for providing a row of chairs in the shade for the family instead of just the one that she herself required.

But as the judge came closer, she was struck by how really old he looked. His skin had a gray tinge, and he seemed to be panting a little in exertion. She realized that he was no longer the robust patriarch who had cast everyone she loved out of his life as if they'd never been. She could *almost* pity him. And she certainly wouldn't deny an old man a bit of cool shade on a hot August afternoon. Besides, after today she'd never have to see or speak to him again.

Maggie rose slowly and went to meet the two men. She had no smile for Elijah Foley, but she managed to tell him quite civilly, "This way, Grandfather—it's cooler under the canopy." It was the first time in her entire life that she'd addressed her mother's father by that name. But he *had* come, for which she was realizing she grudgingly respected him, and he was playing the role of Bryan's kin. For that, and for the sake of the watching eyes all around, she called him "Grandfather."

"Thank you, Margaret," he replied in that haughty, sonorous voice of his. She thought with an odd feeling of unreality that here was another first. Never in her memory had Elijah Foley addressed her directly, let alone by her Christian name.

Continuing to display the courtesy that she knew the occasion demanded, Maggie forced herself to extend her hand to the old man. He ceased leaning on Mac Manero and grasped her slim fingers in his gnarled ones. His hand shook at first, but then he gripped a bit harder and that seemed to steady him.

Maggie gave Mac Manero a dismissing look. "Thank you," she said coolly, "for your help."

"Anytime." Mac nodded, a slow smile playing around his mouth. He returned to his place with the other mourners.

Maggie led her grandfather to a chair. She helped him to sit down. Then it was time for the final ceremony to begin. Flanked by her only childhood friend on one side and the man who had disowned her and those she loved most on the other, Maggie Durrant listened as the minister read from the Twenty-third Psalm.

"Thou preparest a table before me in the presence of mine enemies...."

Maggie heard the well-known words only vaguely. Her mind was on the stiff-backed old man sitting next to her. There was no doubt about it now. Her defiant gesture of giving Bryan a splendid funeral had backfired. She was finding herself shamed at people's kindness and forced, for decency's sake, to sit beside the one man she could never forgive. She decided that if she could get through this day, she could get through anything.

Maggie added a single white rose to the lush flower arrangement on the fine casket. The minister said a final prayer. Then the time had come for the improvised potluck at the old Sluicer's Bar schoolhouse down the hill.

Allison, who knew what it cost Maggie to maintain a pretense of civility toward the old man, turned to the judge as soon as the ceremony ended and offered him her hand.

"Judge Foley, let me help you down to the schoolhouse. There'll be refreshments there."

Elijah replied that he felt tired and would go directly to his car. Maggie experienced some relief. She dreaded the potluck, but she dreaded having the judge there even more.

When the old man was up and leaning on Allison, he said very stiffly, "Good day, then, Margaret."

"Yes, Grandfather," Maggie said. "Goodbye."

Allison led him away.

Once her friend and the old man disappeared beyond the cemetery gate, Maggie stood. She accepted a hug and a few soft words of understanding from Odetta Lafray, who owned the coffee shop in Brandy City where Maggie's mother had once worked. Then Maggie strolled with the crowd down the unpaved access road. They proceeded to the landmark building that had once been the Sluicer's Bar schoolhouse and was now used as a community center.

Inside there was no question of the purpose for which the structure had been intended. Black chalkboards still lined the walls. The old wood floors were scuffed from the soles of hundreds of little shoes. There remained a few old one-armed pine desks beneath the tall many-paned double-hung windows.

Two long tables had been set up near the front of the room. They were covered with paper cloths and weighted down with favorite casseroles.

For about the hundredth time Maggie said, "Thank you for coming, Bryan would have appreciated it." Then she grimly went forward to claim a paper plate.

She loaded it up and took a soda from the big washtub full of ice and cold drinks. Then she went outside to sit beneath the cedar trees, where she graciously received a long string of sympathetic little speeches.

Surprisingly enough, she found she appreciated hearing the timeworn phrases of comfort from the people of the town. The men and women of Brandy City and Sluicer's

Bar were the very ones she'd thought she could never get far enough away from fifteen years before.

But now, from a more mature perspective, they seemed kinder than she remembered and more tolerant. At first, realizing this shamed her. But as she let herself relax a little, she found she could simply accept this new view of them and take solace from their thoughtfulness. Of course, Maggie would never choose to actually make her home in a small town like this. But she could see now that, as a wounded young girl, she'd judged them all much too harshly.

"I hate this town," she used to insist to her mother all those years ago. "The way they all talk about us. You know what they call us, those *Dreamin' Durrants*...."

"Never mind." Julie Durrant's voice had been so gentle. "You're young. There's much kindness here. But the life I've given you hasn't allowed you to see it...."

"You seem to be holding up pretty well." The deep voice from behind Maggie put an abrupt end to her memories of the past.

Maggie took a strengthening breath. For the past hour or so she'd actually managed to put Mac Manero from her mind. Obviously he wasn't about to let her go on like that.

Keeping her voice noncommittal, she said, "People are being very kind."

He dropped into the folding chair beside her as if he'd been invited. "That's what I love about living here. People *care*. And they're not afraid to show it."

She looked at him, using her most direct and intimidating stare. "Everyone's been very nice." Her voice was without expression. She was trying by complete unresponsiveness to get him to go away. It was a technique she often employed if a man seemed too interested in her. Usually it got rid of them fast.

"Come on, Maggie. Give it up. It isn't going to work on me." He spoke in a lowered tone, one that stroked along her nerves like a physical caress.

She found herself looking at his big hands, which rested on the aluminum arms of the chair. The thought came, all unbidden, of what it might feel like to have those hands on her skin.

She shifted, crossing her legs, willing such dangerous and tempting thoughts away. "Excuse me? I don't understand what you mean."

He looked at her legs briefly in their black nylon stockings, and then up into her face. "I said you're not having much success at scaring me off."

"I'm not?" She went on looking at him, willing herself not to show any of the attraction she was feeling.

"None at all."

"How about if I just come right out and say it, then?" Her voice was very calm. She was pleased with it, considering the chaos her emotions were in.

"Try it," he said.

"Please leave me alone. I'm not—" she had to seek the word "—interested."

"In men in general, or in me specifically?"

"Either. Both."

He was quiet for a moment. Then he asked, "That's really how you feel?"

Maggie nodded. She didn't trust herself to speak. She had the most absurd and desperate wish that he would not take no for an answer, no matter how many times she said it. She had thought earlier that day that she hated her grandfather and that she hated this man. Right now she despised herself for not even knowing her own mind.

Mac Manero said, "All right, Maggie. If that's really what you want."

Maggie cleared her throat, conscious of the most crushing sense of loss, of a main chance missed. She was sure that it was only the upheaval of the day that made her feel that way. Her brother was dead; she'd just seen him buried. Her emotions were all out of proportion as a result. That was all.

"Yes," she said. "That's what I want."

He was quiet again. He possessed great charm and the grace of a born politician, but she also sensed within him a deep well of pride. He was the kind of man a woman could only say no to so many times before he'd simply accept her decision and walk away. For a man like him, there would always be others more willing.

"All right, then." He rose from the chair and smiled politely down at her. "I wish you the best, Maggie. I know you deserve it."

"Thank you."

He turned and left her.

Maggie found after he was gone that she could no longer sit still. She realized that people were beginning to make their excuses and go on their way. So Maggie went into the schoolhouse again and asked Netty Beach if she could help with anything.

"Don't be silly, Margaret. The whole point is that you don't have to trouble yourself." Netty asked where she would like the remaining food taken.

As gracefully as she could, Maggie explained her circumstances and asked if Netty would distribute the food among everyone who'd helped out.

"Why, I think I can manage that," Netty said.

Maggie thanked the older woman and then found the minister to convey her appreciation and press a donation into his hand.

Then she went out into the late-afternoon sun. The ostentatious limousine she'd hired was waiting for her in the flat by the turn to the bridge. The driver was all ready to take her back to her room in town.

She said, "I think I'd like to go somewhere else first. Is that okay?" Her own voice surprised her with its unaccustomed hesitancy.

The driver tossed her a look through the window that separated them. "You're the boss, ma'am."

She pointed down the bramble-lined road that led to the house where she'd grown up. "That way. Go slowly. I'll tell you when to stop."

The driver started up the car and went where she'd told him to go.

Maggie directed the driver to the clear space by the house where she'd been raised. Once there, she sat for a long while in the back seat of the limousine. She felt sad— and somehow edgy with yearning.

She looked out the side window, her gaze moving from the old house to the beautiful new one across the creek and back to the old one again.

She let her mind wander, thinking that to her the old house had never really been Bryan's. To her the house would always belong to her mother. It had been left to Julie by her own mother, Olivia Foley, who had refused to meekly follow suit when her husband disinherited their only child. Olivia had left all of her own property to Julie when she died. True to form, Harry Durrant had gone through the small fortune in just a few years. But Julie had managed to hold on to the house.

And now Bryan had lost the house, too. The man on the hill owned it.

Maggie glanced again at the graceful new house across the creek. Was Mac Manero up there even now, watching her from those tall windows? Was he wondering just what she was up to, sitting there in the showy rented limousine, staring at his house after she'd told him a half hour before that she wanted nothing to do with him?

In all honesty, Maggie admitted, she was wondering the same thing herself.

She looked back through all the overgrown bushes at her mother's house, and at that moment the answer came to her.

She wanted the old house for herself. She just couldn't bear the idea of the house belonging to someone else.

It was totally crazy for her to feel that way, really, and Maggie knew it. She never intended to live in Sluicer's Bar; she could hardly wait to get Bryan's affairs in order and hustle back to Arizona and her *real* life. But at the same time her heart refused to accept the thought of a stranger owning her mother's house.

Maggie spoke to the patient driver, telling him she was ready to return to town. He started up the engine and took her back.

In her motel room she turned on the air conditioner, took off her dress and lay down on the bed wearing her slip. As the room cooled, she rested from all the stress of the past few hours and soon fell asleep.

When she woke, it was dark. Her travel clock said it was past nine. The room was cold.

Maggie shut off the air conditioner and opened the windows. Since the motel was right on the river, the rushing sound of it came in with the night air. Two days ago the sound had seemed to mock her, but now it was soothing and beautiful once more.

There was still settling up to do, but she felt that the worst was behind her. In a week, if she could manage it, she planned to depart Brandy City with all of her brother's debts paid and his affairs in order. She also wanted to leave with possession of her mother's house.

There was only one way to get that, she knew. She'd have to deal with the owner. But really, she'd have to speak with him again anyway, because she fully intended to reimburse him for the money her brother had owed him.

She'd been hasty and tactless, she realized now, in freezing Mac out before their dealings with each other were finished. On the other hand, though, that could work out for the best. They were clear with each other now that nothing was going to happen between them.

Maggie took the phone book from beneath the Gideon Bible by the bed. She found Mac Manero's number and she dialed it.

In the back of her mind some wiser self chuckled softly, whispering that what she wanted from Mac Manero had nothing to do with real estate. Maggie ignored that wiser self.

She wanted her mother's house. Mac Manero owned it. She had no choice but to deal with him.

Three

***

When Mac entered the dim, rustic interior of Farley's Steak House on Main Street the next night, he knew exactly where to look for her. Not down in front by the big wall of windows overlooking the river. But in the enclosed, private booths in the back.

He was right. She sat in a booth along the wall that separated the restaurant from the bar. There was a tall bottle of beer sweating on the varnished pine table in front of her.

As he approached her, he could see the curve of her hip beneath the table. She was dressed in a red shirt and a slim-fitting tan skirt. She'd let her dark hair down in back but kept it off her face with the aid of two combs. Her huge, brandy-colored eyes watched him as he came near.

As he slid in opposite her, she murmured grimly, "Thank you for coming."

The waitress appeared. Mac called her by name and asked for a beer. Then the two of them sat, sizing each other up. His beer came, and they each ordered a steak.

"How about some wine?" Mac suggested before the waitress left them. "The cabernet is good."

Maggie shook her head. "Beer's fine."

After the waitress moved on, they stared at each other some more, and then Mac grew tired of that. Beneath her wary reserve, that core of vulnerability still reached out to him.

What the hell, he thought. I'm having dinner with a pretty woman. So she's got a bad attitude when it comes to men. No reason I have to give her more evidence that she's right.

He allowed himself to smile. She watched his mouth, her own full lips softening just a little. He knew then for sure that whatever she'd said the day before, she *was* interested. She just didn't *want* to be interested.

It was going to be his job to convince her it was safe to be interested. Considering her strength and determination, that wasn't going to be easy. Mac decided he'd always enjoyed a challenge.

He said, "I'm glad you called me."

Her full mouth grew tight again. "This isn't a social occasion. I want to talk to you about a...business matter."

"All right." He kept his voice bland. "But that's no reason we can't share an enjoyable meal, is it?"

She considered that, looking at him sideways as if his question might have been some sort of trick. "Well, no, of course not."

He wanted to tell her to relax, but then he decided that that was what every man who'd ever managed to get within three feet of her must have said. He knew he wasn't going to get through to her by doing what other men did.

"So this is strictly a business dinner, is that what you're telling me?" he asked her.

She looked away and then back at him. "Yes."

"You want to make me a business proposition?"

"More or less."

"You're not going to do that before we've even had our salads, are you?"

She *almost* smiled. "No, that would be bad business."

"Right. You need to butter me up a little first."

She caught her full bottom lip in her teeth and then immediately released it—as if she'd suddenly realized that the gesture might be construed as provocative.

"I mean," he hastened to add, "you want me to be receptive, don't you?"

She was looking at him sideways again. "What are you getting at?"

"Ways you could butter me up." He hurried on before she could start formulating negative assumptions again. "Let's see. You could beg to hear my life story. Every man likes to brag about himself, in case you didn't know. And the great thing about that angle is, it hardly requires any effort from you. Just act impressed at how far I've come. I do all the talking. You just sit there, smile every once in a while and say 'Oh, Mac, how wonderful of you' every now and then. I'll probably sign any piece of paper you wave in front of me and then go home a happy man."

She actually chuckled. "Somehow I doubt you'd be taken in by a woman gushing over your accomplishments."

"It's only one suggestion," he said.

"And the others?" She took a sip from her beer.

"Well, we could talk about the weather. Or movies. How about politics? There's the burning question of whether the new levee measure will pass at the county board of supervisors meeting the week after next or not."

"You're on the board of supervisors, then?" She asked the question as if it were something she'd assumed all along.

He tipped his beer at her. "Two terms running."

"I thought you would be, from what you said yesterday after the funeral, about loving this town—and how people here really care. It's pretty obvious you're a real town booster, so it makes sense that local politics would be important to you." She shifted in her seat, rearranging her skirt. For a moment she leaned toward him, and he got a whiff of the musky scent she used, mingled with that indefinable something that was only her.

A lambent flare of anticipation flickered up within him. Mac savored the feeling. At that moment Mac admitted to himself that he would probably put up with a lot for the chance to make love with Maggie Durrant.

She interrupted the erotic turn of his thoughts with a mundane question. "Where are you from originally?"

He lifted a teasing eyebrow at her. "You *do* want to hear my life story, then?"

But she refused, as usual, to tease back. When she spoke, it was in a businesslike tone. "I admit I'm curious about you. You own my mother's house now. And you seem to have known my brother as well as anyone did."

"I was born in Los Angeles. East L.A., to be specific," he said in answer to her question.

"A rough area, from what I've heard," she said.

"It's worse now, but it was pretty rowdy there then, too," he told her. "My father was Mexican, Puerto Rican and Apache. My mother was Swedish, Irish and Italian."

He grinned. "I'm a mutt," he told her cheerfully. "As American as pizza pie and pocket tacos." He felt a flush of triumph as he watched a little smile tug on her mouth. He was finally succeeding in amusing her. He added, "Now *you* say, 'Oh, Mac, how fascinating....'"

She laughed, a throaty sound. It was the first time he'd heard her laugh. Mac let the sound wash over him, pleased all out of proportion that he'd been the one to coax it from her.

"Do your folks still live there, in southern California?" she asked.

"No, they're dead."

"Oh." Her big eyes held compassion. Mac thought it a great improvement over wariness.

The waitress came with their salads then. For a few minutes they busied themselves with the food.

Then Maggie said, "What happened to them?"

"My parents?"

"Yes—I mean, if you don't mind telling me."

"It's not a happy story, Maggie."

"I'd like to hear it."

Mac told the old story quickly. It wasn't something he told everyone, but it was not a secret, either.

"I had an older brother, Ritchie. He got mixed up with a bad group of kids. Evidently they'd formed some kind of juvenile burglary ring, and they were breaking in and robbing middle-class houses in the San Fernando Valley and Glendale. I *think* my brother cheated on his own partners, at least that's what I was told when I tried to piece it together later. His partners came after him at home. My mother and father were there, too. I was a few blocks away at a friend's house."

"They were all killed?" Maggie asked. Mac nodded. "Did the police catch the killers?"

Mac shook his head. "There wasn't enough evidence to bring anyone to trial."

Maggie pushed her salad plate away. It was only half-finished.

"It was a long time ago," he said softly.

She raised her chin, and her eyes were overly bright. "That doesn't make it any less tragic."

"Sometimes you have to just let things go, Maggie."

"You're telling me you never so much as *thought* of revenge?" Even in the dim restaurant light, he could see two spots of color high up on her cheeks. As he'd suspected, Maggie Durrant wasn't the kind to look tolerantly on injustice.

"Of course I thought of revenge," he said. "No thirteen-year-old in the history of man has ever been so full of vengeful thoughts as I was."

"So what did you do?"

"I got into real estate."

She narrowed her eyes at him. "What does that have to do with revenge?"

"My mother's brother was very wealthy—a big land developer in the San Fernando Valley. Uncle Victor took me in. He also took me under his wing. I bought my first house, a fixer-upper in Highland Park, when I was sixteen."

"I don't understand. You mean you forgot right away about the murder of your family?"

"No. I took a lesson from Ritchie. I learned that, first and foremost, I needed *not* to be like him. Ritchie had no power. He was just another kid with a chip on his shoulder who thought he had it all figured out."

"You idolized him, didn't you?" she asked quietly.

"He was my big brother," Mac said, a little nonplussed at the way she'd cut through his adult objectivity to the heart of the matter. That had been the hardest part of the whole nightmare for the thirteen-year-old Mac to accept; that the brother he'd worshiped had got himself and their parents killed.

Mac went on with the story. "Uncle Victor let me run a little wild for a while, until I'd managed to find out who all of Ritchie's partners were. Then one night, when I got back to his house way past midnight as usual, he confronted me. He called me in his study and he locked the door and he told me if I thought I was man enough to avenge my family, then I should be man enough to face my own pain. I tried at first to pretend I didn't know what he meant, but I knew. Grief was eating me alive, and Uncle Victor saw that. Neither of us left that room until I broke down and let it all out."

Mac took another sip of his beer.

Maggie asked, "And then what?"

"And then he made a deal with me."

Their steaks came, grilled to charbroiled perfection, but Maggie ignored hers.

"What was the deal?" she asked eagerly the minute the waitress had left them.

"I would wait five years, finish high school and learn what my uncle could teach me, as well. And then, if I still wanted to, whatever it took, he'd help me go after them."

A knowing look crossed Maggie's face. "I get it." She picked up her knife and fork. "Within five years you'd grown out of the need for revenge."

Mac laughed, a not altogether pleasant sound. "No, Maggie. I'm hardly *that* noble."

"Then what?"

"At the end of five years there was no one to get. There were three of them. One was dead. One was doing life in prison for killing a police officer. The third had been in a bad fight and taken a knife in the back. He was paralyzed from the waist down." Mac cut a piece of meat and brought it to his mouth. He added, before eating, "Fate took care of them for me. Uncle Victor was a very wise man."

"He's dead, too?"

Mac nodded. "Not long ago. Peacefully. In his sleep."

"You were his heir?"

"No. He had five children of his own, all grown by the time he took me in. He left his fortune to them and *their* children. To me, he gave much more than money. He gave me love and a new start." Mac allowed himself a smile. "And, of course, he cosigned my first loan."

Maggie smiled back at him, her eyes a little misty. Mac thought of what he'd wanted on the porch of her mother's house three days before. Then he'd hungered for another glimpse of the secret softness in her eyes. He was getting his glimpse right now.

However tough and defensive she might be on the outside, he could see that Maggie Durrant had a tender, compassionate heart. Mac liked that. Beyond the way she intrigued him, even beyond the way she stirred his senses, he was beginning to *like* her.

The waitress appeared to ask them if their steaks were all right. Maggie said hers was wonderful and started right in to prove it by eating with complete concentration.

Mac complimented the food as well and then ordered two more beers. Neither of them spoke for a while as the food disappeared from their plates. The waitress brought their drinks and left with the empties.

Mac finished his steak and sat back.

Maggie looked up, just finishing her own dinner. "Still hungry?" she asked. Her question reminded him that she considered herself the hostess for this meal.

On the phone she'd been painfully clear about her intention of picking up the tab. Maggie Durrant was no fool. She knew that the one who paid most often called the shots.

"I've had plenty." Mac smiled back at her, admiring her shining, coffee-colored hair and the oval shape of her face. She possessed a beauty that was both exotic and earthy. Mac thought it would be hard to get bored looking at a face like hers.

"Dessert, then?" she asked.

"Just coffee."

Maggie signaled the waitress, who took their empty plates and brought the coffee. Maggie then wrapped her hands around her mug, but didn't drink from it. She stared down into the rising steam.

Mac realized it was well past the time for her to tell him what she was after.

The waitress passed by again, this time with a thank-you and the check. Maggie grabbed the little tray before it hit the table. Mac hid his smile. He'd let her take comfort in whatever power paying for dinner gave her.

She surprised him when she spoke. "So, what made you come to Brandy City?"

Mac let himself gloat just a little before answering her question. Rather than getting down to business, she was asking more about him. However things had started out between them, she was avoiding letting them end.

He said, "That's a good question. I suppose, since I started out on the mean streets of a big city, I always dreamed about someplace better, where people were kinder. I used to imagine there might be a place where everyone would know everyone else. A place where people looked out for each other and where a family being destroyed by a bunch of wild kids wasn't likely to happen. I came through here on a camping trip fifteen years ago, and three years later I bought the Langdon place up on Veneration Hill. I lived there until I built my house in Sluicer's Bar two years ago.''

Maggie stirred her coffee, still not drinking it. "Brandy City is your dream come true, then?'' The thread of cynicism in the question was unmistakable.

Mac reached across the varnished table and gently stilled her hand, which had been stirring pointlessly. With a single quick, sharp breath, she looked up at him.

Her slim wrist was warm in his grip. He could feel her pulse beneath his thumb. She didn't pull away, but her eyes had become guarded once more.

Mac asked, though he already knew the answer, "Why the cynicism, Maggie?''

Her gaze didn't waver. "I had dreams, too. As a kid. I dreamed of getting as far away from Brandy City as I could, and then never coming back. It looks like you and I have always been going in the opposite directions.''

He smiled. "Until we met. In the middle.''

"This isn't the middle. This is the place I came from. I don't live here anymore. I live in Phoenix. I have a nice, modern, Spanish-style house with a red tile roof and a bougainvillea climbing the side fence. I smile and say hello to my neighbors on either side, but I wouldn't know their names if they weren't written on their mailboxes. And you know what?'' She pulled her wrist from his grip. "I like it that way.''

Mac shrugged and finished his coffee. "If you say so.''

Maggie put several bills on the check tray. "Let's go, all right?'' She rose quickly and stood at the end of the booth, eager to be gone.

He looked at her. "Where to?''

"Let's take a walk by the river. We'll finish this up.''

He didn't like the final way she said that. He looked down at her high-heeled sandals. They were hardly appropriate for climbing over the rocks on the riverbank.

Maggie saw his doubtful expression and permitted herself a smile. "Don't worry. I'll take them off." For the briefest moment, in the winsome curve of her mouth, he was reminded of Bryan.

Then she was turning and walking away from him. He rose quickly and followed her out to the street.

Outside it was nearly dark. They walked without speaking along the covered sidewalk, nodding occasionally and murmuring greetings whenever they encountered someone they knew.

Brandy City lay in a pocket of high pine-covered hills. Like Sluicer's Bar, it had sprung up during the gold rush, and still owed a portion of its industry to the gold trade. Panning and dredging continued to bring in tourists every summer, though most of the great hardrock mines of the area had closed down.

The town was built along two rivers, which flowed together at the west end of town. Bridges joined the banks at intervals, three along the Brandy and one across the Yuba just past the point where the Yuba swallowed the Brandy and the two rivers became one.

Maggie led Mac over the central bridge across the Brandy. They passed her motel and continued up Mercantile Street to the bend in the road that led out of town. They went by the Methodist church, where Bryan's final service had been held the day before.

Fine old Victorian houses lined the west side of the street. One of them, gray with white gingerbread trim, belonged to Judge Elijah Foley. Maggie walked past it as if it weren't even there.

Where the houses ended, at the bend in the road, they came to the steep bank that led down to the Yuba. They turned the corner and strolled another hundred yards. There Maggie shucked off her sandals. Then they began picking their way down the rocks to the water's edge.

"Welcome to the town swimming hole," she told him somewhat jauntily, tossing out an arm to indicate the high slate crags on the other side, the small beach and the lazily rippling surface of the green river. Then she looked the slightest bit sad. "Or at least it used to be, way back when I was a kid."

"It still is," he reassured her, thinking for the first time that Brandy City and what happened there meant more to Maggie than she wanted to admit to herself. "Mostly for the kids. They like to swim here because they can park their cars up on the road and leave all the doors open and their car radios going full blast." He snorted. "Drives all us grown-ups crazy."

The sandy beach was surrounded on either side by jutting beds of slate rock. Agile as a cat, even in her pencil-thin skirt, Maggie climbed the slate and sat down. Mac joined her. They sat for a few minutes, sharing the twilight and watching the occasional swooping shadows of the bats that dived for insects above the surface of the water.

Maggie asked, "How did you end up with my mother's house?"

He understood that she was edging up to her reason for calling him. He explained, "I told you I made my money in real estate. On a smaller scale that's what I do here."

"Buy and sell property, you mean?"

"Not exactly. What I've bought here I'm keeping. I own six houses now, including the one I live in. And have you noticed the pizza parlor by the Courthouse Bridge?" She nodded. "That's mine, too. I have a manager running that, but the rest of the properties I manage myself." He chuckled. "I've developed skills I never knew I had since coming here."

She looked at him. "Like what?"

"I'm a demon with a plumber's snake. And you ought to see me replace a worn-out light switch." He waited for her polite chuckle and then returned to the real subject. "Everyone in town knows I'm buying if they want to sell.

"About six months after your mother died, Bryan approached me. He said he needed capital for work on the mine that belonged to your father." Beside him he felt Maggie stiffen. He went on, "Bryan said it had always been his dream to make the Hard Luck Lady pay."

Maggie spoke then, her voice thick with disdain she didn't bother to mask. "My father had the same dream. Every penny he could get his hands on went into that mine—*or* into the cash register at the St. Regis bar." She waved her hand in front of her face, shooing away a persistent mosquito. Then she said tartly, "So you bought the house from him."

"Yes."

"For a rental property?"

"No, actually the house is in pretty bad shape." Maggie looked away at that comment, but said nothing. Mac continued, "I bought it for the land. I was planning my own house at the time, and I thought the property would make a good access. I could build a new bridge there and not have to go all the way around across Stoney Creek and Woodman Creek and in the back way like I do now. But I was pretty absorbed with the plans for my own house at the time. And Bryan asked to rent from me until I got ready to bring in the wreckers—"

Without warning, Maggie was on her feet. She turned and fled down the rocks, but pulled herself up short when she reached the sand. She went to the water's edge and stood there, looking across at the jagged shadows of slate. She held her shoulders stiffly erect.

Mac waited, sure now that she was going to make him an offer for her mother's house. Maggie Durrant was one smart woman. But her mind, Mac sensed, was at war with her heart. She said all she wanted was to get out of town and back to Arizona—yet the idea of his tearing down her mother's house had made her bolt like a wounded deer.

Mac leaned back on his hands and stretched his feet out in front of him, respecting her privacy while she brought herself into control.

Several minutes later she returned to him, her bare feet sure on the rocks. She stood over him, silhouetted against the night sky.

"I want my mother's house," she said blankly. "I suppose you know that." A slight wind rose up and blew her hair around her shoulders. Though her face was hard to see, the shape of her body was tall and proud.

Mac considered. He knew she would be willing to pay well for the house and the acre it sat on. The bridge he'd been planning would end up causing no end of headaches when it came to building permits, anyway. And it hadn't turned out to be such a hardship, after all, to take the back way around to get to his own house.

But neither the money, the trouble of building a bridge, nor the property were the real issues for him. The real issue was Maggie—what was best for her and what would increase his chances with her.

Mac understood that whatever they might share couldn't be forever. He and Maggie would have several strikes against them from the start, since they wanted very different things from life. But then *nothing* was forever; he'd learned that at the age of thirteen when he lost his family.

Mac was sure they could be good for each other for as long as it might last.

"How much do you want for the house?" she demanded.

His thoughts were suddenly very primitive. *You, all of you, tonight* . . . But Mac Manero was a civilized man.

He asked, "What would you do with it if I sold it to you?"

"That's my business."

Mac stood up. "You forget," he retorted as he brushed off his jeans, "I have to live across from that house. It's bad enough now, but in a year or two, with a few good snows, the roof's going to go. Do you think I look forward to watching that house cave in over the next few years?"

"I'll take care of it," she said.

"Right. I'm sure you'll be dropping in from Arizona often."

"I can hire someone."

"Who?"

"Lucius Clay does work like that. And his sister-in-law, Allison, is an old friend of mine."

He shook his head. "I don't like it."

"Lucius is *good*," she argued. "You must have heard of him."

"I know his work, and he *is* good. As a matter of fact, he often works for me," Mac said. "But I'm not talking about Lucius Clay. I'm talking about you."

Maggie stood on a hump of rock, slightly above him. Beyond her head the stars slowly brightened as night laid its claim on the Sierra sky. "What do you mean, you're talking about me?" Her voice was tight as a wound-up spring.

"I don't think it would be good for you," he said frankly. "I have this feeling you would only be holding on to something you'd be better off letting go."

For a moment she said nothing. When she did speak, it was with glacial coldness. "What you feel means nothing to me, Mr. Manero. I hardly even know you. You have absolutely *no right* to tell me what is good for me. *I* decide that—no one else. Is that clear?"

If he'd ever wondered why such a good-looking woman as this remained unspoken for, Mac wondered no more. Maggie Durrant could be as cold as a dead snake when she chose to.

Mac said. "Fine. Let me put it this way, then—no."

"You won't sell me the house?" Her voice was blatantly pugnacious.

"Right. No." He handed her the sandals and shoulder bag that she'd left on the rocks beside him.

She grabbed them sharply and stood for a moment, glaring at him. Then her shoulders slumped a little. She slid around him and made for the steep bank that led to the road. He followed her. Neither of them spoke until they stood on the side of the highway.

She paused to put on her sandals again. The process was a little more involved than removing them, because she needed to brush the sand from her feet.

Mac said, "Here, lean on me," fully expecting her to refuse.

But she surprised him by murmuring a thank-you and bracing a hand on his shoulder. When she was done, she brushed off her hands.

"I apologize for the way I behaved just now," she said stiffly. "It took me off guard, that you plan to tear the house down."

"I understand," Mac said.

Maggie forced a smile. "Look, can we try this conversation again?" She nervously resettled the strap of her bag over her shoulder.

Mac considered her request, then shook his head. "Let it go. You were right, it's not my business what's good for you. In the end my only motivation for selling you that property would be personal."

She looked beyond him, toward the silvery three-quarter moon that hovered just above the mountains. "Because you're attracted to me?"

"Right. Could you live with that, Maggie? Knowing you got your mother's house back because the man who owned it wanted to sleep with you?"

She shook her head, still avoiding his eyes and staring at the moon. "I guess not." She shifted her focus then, and their gazes locked. "Nothing can happen between us," she said.

"Why?" Mac allowed huskiness into the question. He wanted to communicate to her that, were they to be lovers, she would not be the only one made vulnerable.

"There are a thousand reasons."

"Name one."

Her response came without hesitation. "I'm not looking for anything casual, and yet, with you that's all it could ever be."

Holding her gaze, Mac reached out and touched her. He was careful to move very slowly, as a man who wished to stroke a wild thing would move.

Lightly he traced the line of her jaw. She allowed him the touch, and he felt her shiver a little against the sensitive pads of his fingers. Then he cupped the back of her neck, sliding his hand beneath the midnight fall of her hair. Her nape was warm and soft against his palm.

Something tightened down inside him, and he knew that Maggie Durrant would not leave Brandy City without having known his hands on every inch of her body.

He said, "All right. Maybe it wouldn't be for the rest of our lives. That doesn't mean it would be casual. Does this feel casual to you?"

Two cars whizzed past on the highway, whipping up eddies of dust that swirled around them and then settled again. When the cars were gone, Maggie said, "Please take your hand away, MacEvan. I want to go back to the motel now."

Mac dropped his arm, aware that the side of the highway was no place to pursue this intimate matter.

"Let's go," he said. They began walking.

They strolled past the church and the Victorian homes without speaking. When they reached her motel, he followed her up the stairs to the landing and her second-floor room.

She turned at the door. "There's just one more thing," she said.

His sigh of relief was practically audible. He had been wracking his brain for a way to keep her from saying goodnight.

"Name it."

"How much did my brother owe you in rent?"

Mac shrugged, trying to look unconcerned. He knew damned well what she was planning, and he thought it way out of line. She wasn't responsible for her brother's bad debts.

"It wasn't that much," he said.

"Fine," she replied. "How much?"

"Look, if he hadn't stayed in the house, it would have just been sitting vacant, anyway. It wasn't in any shape to rent."

"How much, Mac?" She was getting that recalcitrant gleam in her eyes again.

Mac decided it wasn't worth tangling with her about. Especially when he didn't want to tangle with her at all, unless it was on cool sheets in a wide bed.

"How far behind was he?" she demanded.

"Four months." It had been over a year.

"How much was he paying a month?"

Mac named a figure.

Maggie turned and opened the door of her room. "Come in, and I'll write you a check."

Beyond the door Mac spied a big bed. A slow smile widened his mouth. With no hesitation he followed her inside.

Four

As soon as they were inside, Maggie realized her mistake. Allowing herself to be alone with Mac Manero in a room with a closed door was the last thing she should have done.

The two of them stood just inside the door, between a mirrored low dresser and the foot of the bed. Distracted by forbidden desires, Maggie zoomed her attention in on their side-by-side reflections in the mirror, thinking absurdly that they were a couple of giants since neither of their heads would fit into the reflection.

"You all right, Maggie?" Mac asked, his voice threaded with that lazy humor that she had started to thoroughly enjoy—against her own better judgment.

Give him the check, she told herself firmly, and then he can go.

"Have a seat," she said.

He dropped to the end of the bed, which took up over half the small room, anyway. With Mac sitting on it, one big leg drawn up and laid across the other knee, the bed appeared to expand to swallow everything. Now the room seemed *all* bed.

All through dinner she had vacillated. Her good sense kept reminding her that she'd only called him because of the house. Her silly heart wanted to pretend that she was a woman like any other woman, out for an evening with a man who set her pulse racing.

It was much worse at the river. Her emotions had gone haywire. She'd blown her hopes for getting the house back by overreacting when he'd told her he planned to tear it down. And now, after what he'd said about only selling her the house because he desired her, she knew she could never take it from him, anyway.

Maggie saw that she was going to have to accept the inevitable. Her mother's house was lost to her. Strangely enough there was some relief in admitting that she was going to have to let the house go.

But there was no relief in anything else—certainly not in the compelling dark eyes of the man on her bed, or the memory of his touch on the back of her neck. His fingers had been so warm and gentle, curving to cup her head. Right there on the side of the road, where anyone might have seen, she'd longed to let her body sway against his, to lift her mouth up in invitation. . . .

"Something wrong?" Mac grinned at her from the end of the bed, pretending he didn't know exactly the direction of her thoughts.

"No, of course not." She took her checkbook from her purse and crossed to the small round table in the corner beneath the window that looked out on the river below. She pulled the chain on the hanging lamp there and sat down to write out the check.

Mac rose and came up behind her just as she signed her name. She tore the check off the book. The ripping sound grated unbearably loud in the silence between them.

Maggie stood up, turning a little awkwardly to face him in the rather tight space. She held out the check.

He reluctantly reached for it. "I won't deposit it for a while."

"Why not?" Her voice sounded vague to her own ears. Mostly she was thinking of the light brush of his fingers against her knuckles as he took the check from her.

"You might change your mind and decide Bryan's debts aren't your responsibility."

"I won't change my mind. It means a lot to me that he leaves no debts in Brandy City. When my father died, we owed everybody. I hated that. I swore that the next time one of my own died leaving nothing, I'd have enough to settle up. And I do have enough, Mac. I have plenty of money. I've worked damned hard the past fifteen years to make sure of that." Maggie spoke the words quietly, hardly aware that she was revealing more of herself to this man than she had ever exposed to her few casual friends in Phoenix.

Mac had that effect on her, like no one else she'd ever known. He made her want to reveal herself, because she sensed in him the true capacity to understand.

"The thing about money," he said with a tender smile, "is that only the lack of it matters. Once you have it, you learn it's just a tool."

"Did your wise Uncle Victor tell you that?" she asked.

"No, I figured that one out myself."

Maggie found herself smiling back at him. She *did* like him. She liked the power and grace in his big body, she liked the humor he possessed and she liked the way his mind worked. Too bad he just wasn't the man for her—if indeed there was such a thing.

"Cash the check," she instructed. "I want my brother to be paid up in Brandy City. I want everything settled, so I can go back to where I belong."

"Right, Phoenix," he said.

"Yes. I have a good life there."

"So you keep saying."

"Because it's true."

"Right."

She realized it was time to ask him to leave. He wasn't going to sell her back her mother's house, and she'd paid off Bryan's debt to him. Their business together was concluded.

If he would just stop looking at her with those incredible obsidian eyes, she'd tell him where the door was in no uncertain terms. But he didn't stop looking at her.

"You know what I thought, the other day, the first time we met?" he asked.

No, and I don't want to know.... "What?" she asked, her voice ridiculously hushed.

She recalled, though she fought the memory, that frozen moment on the porch of her mother's house. She'd yearned then to feel his arms, a stranger's arms, around her and to rest her head against his chest.

Mac's dark eyes were on her now, and they no longer seemed a stranger's eyes. Maggie's lips felt dry; she moistened them.

"I thought your eyes were soft," he said. "Much softer than you wanted them to be. I wanted to see that again— the softness that you try to hide."

"And have you?" she heard herself asking.

"Yes."

"And what good did it do?"

"Good? I don't know. I only know—"

"Yes?"

"That now I want more."

"It's foolish," she said, shaking her head slowly, unable to break the hold of his gaze but knowing that she should.

"I think you want more, too, if you're honest."

"It's not wise." Her breathy tone failed to convince even herself.

"Be honest, Maggie. Don't you want more, too?"

She kept slowly shaking her head, unable to lie and say no out loud, incapable of telling the truth and becoming more susceptible to him.

He lifted a hand and took her chin gently, just enough to stop the slow shaking of her head. Her skin flamed beneath the touch. "All right, don't say yes," he implored tenderly. "But don't say no, either."

His other hand encircled her waist. She put up no resistance as he pulled her close, the hand on her chin slipping back to cradle her head, guiding it to rest against his chest.

"It feels good just to hold you," he said. He kissed the top of her head, his lips and breath warm in her hair. He breathed her name.

Her impossible wish on the steps of her mother's house had come true. And Mac was right—it felt good. It felt *wonderful,* from the cherishing feel of his hands on her hair to the beat of his heart beneath her ear.

Maggie lifted her face, allowing herself to forget for a moment that she and this man, by his own admission, could create nothing that would endure. He kissed a sweet trail down the center of her forehead, over her nose and right off the end of it to her waiting, eager mouth.

"Oh, my Lord," she heard herself murmuring as his mouth covered hers.

In high summer in the Sierras, a single spark from an untended fire can sweep away whole forests in a sudden explosion of flame. To Maggie, the first touch of Mac's lips on hers felt like that—a flash fire, exploding outward along every nerve to set her whole body ablaze.

Mac groaned against her mouth, feeling the burning heat of the fire, as well. His hands tangled in her loose hair, alternately clutching it and smoothing it down the center of her back. He went on kissing her.

Shamelessly Maggie pressed herself into him, reveling in the deep strength of his chest, the power in his arms and the hardness of his thighs against her own.

His lips roved hers, coaxing and plundering. He nudged at her mouth until she parted for him.

He repeated her name like a chant, over and over as he kissed her. And she kept saying yes, and his name, and then yes again.

She was pure sensation, incapable of thought, and yet she did think. She thought that it was marvelous to feel so alive, to know the exquisite pleasures that her body could know.

She gloried in the roughness of his cheek against her skin. She shuddered at the sweet heat of his breath on her neck before he kissed her there. The rapid beating of his heart against her own made her moan aloud.

Maggie drew in quick, hungry breaths, scenting him and thinking that she would ever after be able to pick him out in total darkness by a kind of instinct without consciously knowing how.

Beneath all this, like the rhythm and flow of life itself, she heard the river out the open window behind her. And it came to her, just as Mac began to pull her toward the bed, that to have found this man here in Brandy City was the ultimate trick of fate.

He took a step backward, then pulled her against him once more. She felt the evidence of his desire at the secret place where her thighs joined. Something melted in her there, at the same time as her mind began to clamor that she must stop this *now*.

She pushed against his chest halfheartedly, and he responded by pulling her closer still and backing one more step toward the bed. His seeking, pleasuring mouth strayed to her neck again, right to the crook where her shoulder began. He nuzzled the collar of her shirt aside and kissed her there, sucking a little. All of her senses were liquid, and she surged up closer to him once more.

She wondered, shocked and aroused, if he would leave a mark there. She thought she should stop him; she had never let any man arouse her the way he was—let alone draw a tiny, telltale bruise on her skin.

She gasped. "Stop, Mac..."

He growled against her neck, but stopped drawing on the flesh there. Instead, his mouth came back to cover hers.

She drowned and burned in desire once more. His hands began tugging her blouse out of her waistband. She managed to free her mouth long enough to protest, but only weakly.

He said against her lips, his voice rough with need, "Some things are destiny, *mi reina,* let it happen, let it be..." His lips strayed to her temples and then to her hair. She heard one of her tortoise-shell combs bounce against the table's edge before dropping to the carpet at their feet.

Mi reina, she thought. How beautiful. She knew a little Spanish; more than one of her employees had been Mexican-American. *Reina* meant queen. He was calling her his queen.

Mac took another step backward. He was almost at the bed. In seconds, she knew with the part of her mind that still reasoned, he would be pulling her down upon it. Once there, she doubted she could summon the will to stop this heady, overpowering magic from finding its natural conclusion.

Beyond the window the river beat over the rocks in a never-ending sigh, as it had all through her girlhood until she'd left this place behind.

"So beautiful," Mac whispered against her hair. "*Muy fuerte,* very strong, and beautiful. I wanted you from the first . . ."

"Mac, I don't think—"

His mouth covered hers again. He kissed her and she kissed him back, and then he began to coax her down to the bed.

"Mac, please . . ."

"Lie down with me, Maggie. Let me love you now . . ."

But Maggie knew in all conscience that she could not. She pushed regretfully but firmly on his shoulders.

He gave in then, as she'd known he would the minute she protested with any force. He dropped to the bed, sliding his hands down her arms as he did so. She was left standing between his open knees, her hands clasped in his.

Neither of them spoke. His head was bent over her hands. She looked down on the black sheen of his hair and the exposed nape of his neck. She yearned to pull his bowed head against her belly, to stroke his coarse black hair, but she knew that would be wrong. This man was not the man for her.

Beyond the window the river rolled on.

After several minutes Mac looked up. He wasn't smiling, but neither did he look angry.

"Okay, Maggie, what now?" he asked. His voice was still woven with rough threads of desire.

Maggie looked into those black eyes. Her heart cried, *Touch me again, please, and never stop....*

Quietly she answered, "Now you have to go."

He looked down again and turned her right hand palm-up. Then he brought it to his mouth. The touch of his lips on her skin caused a hungry shudder all through her.

Mac glanced up sharply, his eyes hot and triumphant at the immediacy of her response to him.

Maggie jerked her hands away, backing out of the dangerous circle of his thighs. "I mean it, Mac. What just happened is all that's ever going to happen."

He shook his head and ran his fingers through his mussed hair. Then he smiled, a rather frightening, feral smile. "I think you lie, *mi reina.*"

"Don't call me that," she snapped.

"Why not?" His smile softened. "It's what my father called my mother." He shook his head. "Funny, I'd forgotten that until tonight. I thought I'd forgotten all my Spanish—my father was the only one who spoke it in our family. And after he was gone, I had no use for it." Mac's face wore a musing expression. "I remember he used to tell me, 'love always sounds better in Spanish, my son.'" Mac looked at Maggie once more. "Wouldn't you like to be my queen?"

Something inside her whispered, *absolutely,* but of course she didn't allow the word to reach her lips. She lied. "No. Please never call me that again."

He stood up. She almost wished he'd sit back down; he was less imposing that way.

He shrugged. "All right, Maggie. I'll never call you that again—at least not until the next time you hold your mouth up for me to kiss."

Maggie swallowed and held her tongue. Just because he baited her didn't mean she had to respond in kind. Also, he was right. She had invited his kiss. She probably deserved a snide remark or two from him after the way she'd behaved.

"I led you on and I was wrong. Now, I'd like you to leave, please."

His blunt features wore no expression. She realized she'd finally succeeded in trying his patience. "I'll go now, but that doesn't end anything," he warned.

"Our business is settled." She bent to scoop up the wrinkled check that he'd dropped unheeded while he drove her wild with his kisses. "You love this town and plan to stay here. I like the big city, where people mind their own affairs. Would you come with me to Phoenix if I asked you?" She held out the check to him.

He took it, looking pained. "Look, Maggie. Give it a little time, would you? We've known each other three whole days."

"Just answer the question."

"Hell, I don't know yet."

"But you know enough to be sure I ought to make love with you."

"It's not the same thing."

"To me," she insisted, "it's exactly the same. Like I said at the river, I'm not looking for a casual affair."

"Damn it, neither am I."

"But if you won't leave Brandy City and I can't stand the thought of living here, then what else have we got?"

It was a moment before he spoke. Then he said, "We've got something that isn't going to disappear just because you've got a problem with men."

"Don't be ridiculous," she shot back too quickly. "I have no problems with men, none whatsoever."

Mac didn't even bother to frame a reply to that. He turned instead and went to the door.

He said good-night and was gone before she could pointedly say "Good*bye*."

The next day, Monday, Maggie faced the unpleasant duty of visiting all of the merchants in town to pay off any tabs Bryan might have run up with them. As she had expected, Bryan's biggest bills were at Brandy City's two bars, the St. Regis and Farley's, adjacent to the steak house.

Most of the debts were over a year old, which didn't surprise Maggie. Bryan would have been flush for a while with the sale of the house, and then begun operating on credit once more. Eventually the credit would have stopped for lack of payment.

As Maggie had discovered at the funeral, people seemed kinder than she remembered. She found herself wondering if it had only been her own childish defensiveness that had made them seem cruel. Each shopkeeper expressed condolences and had a good thing or two to say about Bryan.

Bart Farley even tried to refuse her money.

"Hell, Maggie, Bryan was always good for a laugh or two. He kept things lively. I figure that was worth a few free drinks."

Maggie had insisted Bart let her pay the debt, contending that she was Bryan's sole heir and thus responsible for his obligations. It wasn't much of an argument, really. She hadn't even formally been declared administrator yet, and the most she was going to "inherit" was the mineral rights to the Hard Luck Lady, her father's worthless gold mine.

But Maggie Durrant could be very convincing when she tried. In the end even Bart Farley let her clear her brother's debt.

Late in the afternoon she ran into Allison Clay outside the post office.

"Come on over to Manero's," Allison urged, meaning the pizza parlor by the Courthouse Bridge that had Mac's last name above the door. "Caleb and the kids are giving me the night off from the kitchen. Join us, Maggs. We'd love to have you."

"Give me a rain check," Maggie begged. She'd already been in the pizza parlor once to find out if Bryan owed the place any money. She wasn't going back again. She might run into Mac there.

"I mean it," Allison said. "We have to get together before you leave this time."

"I promise," Maggie reassured her friend, and accepted Allison's loving hug before making her escape.

Later she drove to Del Oro City, twelve miles away, and ate a solitary dinner of rainbow trout and wild rice at the Del Oro Pines Inn. The food was excellent, but she kept thinking pointlessly about how much fun it would have been to share a pizza with the Clays.

Back at her motel room she watched an old movie on television and turned in early.

She had to get up in the middle of the night to shut the window and close out the noise of the river. The low, unending sigh sounded almost like a reproof. It kept weaving into her dreams and waking her up, making her feel as if she'd done something wrong—or turned away something right.

In the morning she rose early. She dressed in old clothes and hiking boots and put her hair in braids, which she anchored in a crown on her head. She stopped in at the gro-

cery store, looking for empty boxes. They'd had deliveries
before dawn, so she filled the back seat and trunk of her
car. She'd need the cartons later in the day to begin the job
of clearing out her mother's house.

She had breakfast at the Gold Pan Café, where her
mother had worked as a waitress after her father died.

Business was slow at the café. Odetta Lafray, the waitress who was also the co-owner, slid in across from Maggie
just as Maggie was finishing up.

Tall and rail-thin, with midnight hair gone steel gray
now, Odetta had been a good friend as well as a fair em-
ployer to Maggie's mother. During Maggie's teenage years,
Odetta had been forever trying to give her a little helpful
advice. Then, Maggie had borne the woman's chatter in
stoic silence, reminding herself that her family owed the
Lafrays a lot for saving them from complete ruin after her
father died.

"Deader'n Andy's corned beef hash in here," Odetta
groaned. Andy was Odetta's husband and the other owner
of the place. Odetta went on to explain that the new Donut
Shoppe by the Mercantile Street bridge, as well as the coffee shop at the bend in the road just outside of town, was
giving them competition for the breakfast trade.

Odetta began wiping down the condiment rack at the
end of the table. "Gotten so we can only afford one other
waitress to help me out in the afternoons," Odetta said.
"We'll probably end up selling out after the first of the
year. We'll get ourselves a trailer and head down your way
to Arizona, where the winters don't freeze the old bones.
Mac Manero's said he's interested in buying us out."
Odetta meticulously polished the metal top of the sugar
dispenser.

Maggie tried to show no response at the mention of
Mac's name. She'd made a big mistake in coming in here,

she realized. She'd forgotten just how bold Odetta could be in her meddling. At the funeral Odetta had been so polite and reserved. And then yesterday, when Maggie had dropped in to pay Bryan's tab, another waitress had been working and Maggie had talked to Andy. But now Odetta had that look: a meddler on the scent of a major opportunity to help two hearts to start beating as one.

Odetta asked, coyly casual, "Heard you and Mac had dinner together, night before last. You two have a nice time?" She put the sugar back and started wiping off the salt.

"Yes, very nice." Maggie said the words resignedly.

"Mac loves this town," Odetta went on. "And he's been one fine supervisor. Yeah, Mac Manero's all right."

Odetta's eyes fairly twinkled. Maggie managed a noncommittal smile, thinking that this was just what she loathed about Brandy City. A woman spent an evening with a man, and everyone for miles around heard wedding bells.

Maggie adjusted the collar of her plaid shirt and told herself that there was no way Odetta could see the slight discoloration on her neck where Mac had kissed her. It was barely visible. It would fade as if it had never been within another day or two.

Eager to be gone before Odetta started demanding to know when the wedding would take place, Maggie put some bills on top of the check and stood up to leave.

Odetta asked very gently, "You all right, Maggie?" Her piercing hazel eyes were full of concern. "You look a bit pushed."

"I'm fine." Maggie's flat tone invited no more questions, even from the persistent Odetta Lafray.

Odetta knew Maggie well. Immediately the older woman's attitude became scrupulously offhand. "So where you headed?'' she asked, sparing a quick glance at Maggie's boots. "Going hiking?''

"Right now I want to go up to the Hard Luck Lady and have a look around.''

"Gonna hike in, then?'' Odetta knew, of course, that Bryan's four-wheel-drive truck had gone into the river with him, but she wouldn't mention that. Odetta Lafray was pushy, but never cruel.

"Yes, it's a pretty walk up there,'' Maggie said.

Odetta snorted. "Pretty steep, is what you mean.''

"The exercise will do me good,'' Maggie replied, then added, "See you.''

Odetta waved goodbye with her cleaning towel.

Twenty minutes later, as Odetta was sitting in a different booth, her back to the door, polishing the last sugar dispenser to a reflective shine, Mac Manero put his hands on her shoulders and bent to kiss her on the cheek.

She chuckled and batted at him with her towel. "Hands off. I'm spoken for.''

"The good ones are always taken,'' Mac groused. Then he took the seat opposite her.

Odetta set the sugar in its place. "The usual?''

"Great.''

"Denver omelet, double hash browns!'' she called over her shoulder.

"You got it!'' Andy shouted from the other room. Then he stuck his head through the service window, wiry gray hair jutting at all angles from under his little chevron cook's cap and greeted Mac.

The two men talked for a few minutes as Odetta poured Mac's coffee and set a large orange juice in front of him. Then Andy disappeared to whip up the omelet.

Mac liked the Lafrays. They always treated him well, and Odetta was a font of information about what was going on in town. Though from lunchtime on their restaurant was in competition with Mac's pizza parlor, the Lafrays didn't let it bother them. So Mac returned the favor. Besides, he knew they were getting older and would probably end up selling out to him eventually, anyway. Then he'd make something else of the place, another kind of business, though he wasn't sure what yet.

Odetta set his food in front of him, waltzed away for a moment and came back with more coffee. He thanked her and began to eat.

She continued to hover near his elbow. Mac swallowed and looked up at her. "Spit it out, Odetta."

"Well, I know it's none of my business," Odetta began.

Mac gestured with his fork at the seat across from him. Odetta slid into it.

"I'm listening," Mac said.

Odetta spoke in a low voice, though there was no one nearby to hear. "Maggie Durrant just left, not half an hour ago."

"So?" Mac made his voice as uninterested as he wanted to feel.

After a wretched, restless night in which every dream had featured Maggie, totally nude and crawling all over him, Mac had decided he'd had about enough of the torture of wanting a woman who was afraid to want him back.

The other night he'd told her that what was between them wasn't going to go away.

By the following morning he'd determined that the *last* thing he needed in his life was a woman who couldn't decide which she despised more: men, or the town he loved.

"Her mother, Julie, used to work for me," Odetta was saying. "So maybe I know Maggie better than lots of folks in town. Maggie didn't have an easy time of it, growing up, if you know what I mean. But she made something of herself in spite of the odds against her."

"I understand," Mac said, keeping his voice bland, waiting for Odetta to get to the point.

"Now none of her people are left but the judge, and the two of them don't even speak. I wouldn't like to see her hurt by anything else or any*one* else around here. Lots of folks in town feel that way."

Mac felt defensive for a moment. Maggie hated Brandy City. Still, people in town were bent on protecting her— from *him*. But then he remembered that he no longer had any intention of pursuing Maggie further, so nothing that Odetta might say would matter. He said in a kindly tone, "You're right, Odetta, it's none of your business."

Odetta shrugged. "It's too late now. You got me started. I'm gonna have my say."

Mac sighed. "All right, Odetta."

"You're lookin' forty in the face," Odetta said. "And you're still a bachelor."

"Is that a crime?"

"It's bad odds is what it is."

"Bad odds for what?"

"If you haven't tied the knot by now, odds are you won't be doing it in the future."

Mac really was starting to feel defensive now, partly because what Odetta said had the ring of truth. Mac enjoyed his bachelorhood; it was a way of life for him. "How do you know I'll never get married?" he heard himself say with more of an edge than he might have intended.

Odetta shrugged again, all the wisdom of her fifty-odd years of life in a small town in her eyes. "You're almost forty, so your hormones aren't giving you orders any-more. You're free to see the reality when romance comes your way."

Mac knew he shouldn't ask, but he did, anyway: "What's the reality?"

"That there's no need to saddle yourself with the trouble and expense of keeping a cow when you can have it all, from butter to ice cream, just by walking down to the corner store."

Mac didn't know whether to laugh or be insulted. Odetta spared him the necessity of either by relenting a little and adding, "But I told her you were all right, anyway."

"Thank you," he said, because he didn't know quite what else to say. Had Maggie been asking about him? Not that it mattered. It didn't matter at all.

"She was in here this morning," Odetta said.

"You said that already."

"Yesterday she was in here to pay up Bryan's tab. She's been all over town doing that, did you know?"

"I heard." And he had, too, in detail, from Bart Farley the night before.

"She left here to hike up to the Hard Luck Lady."

"What for?" He asked the question before he remembered that he didn't care what she was doing.

"She said she wanted to have a look around." Odetta leaned across the table and lowered her voice even further. "I'm worried about her, Mac. She looks drawn tight as a wire, you know what I'm saying? I don't think she's stopped moving since she got the news of poor Bryan's passing. She looks like she could use a good rest. And what's she doing instead? Heading up the side of a mountain on foot all by her lonesome to look over a gold mine that she always begged her mama to get rid of."

Mac suddenly found himself recalling the suffering in Maggie's eyes that first day on the porch of the old house. And the other night, at the river, the bitterness in her voice when she'd spoken of the mine, and the way she'd bolted down the rocks at the news that he planned to tear down her mother's house.

Her actions were the actions of a woman under stress. Odetta was right. She was pushing herself too hard.

But it was no concern of Mac's. She'd made it painfully clear that she needed no help from him. He was going to stay out of it and away from her. A woman like her, with so much pent-up hostility, was bad news for any man.

Odetta volunteered, "The Hard Luck Lady's up behind the county works."

"There's no point in giving me directions, Odetta. I'm not going up there," Mac said.

Odetta grinned, "Well, of course you're not, Mac. Did you think I was hinting you should? Well, I wasn't. Not one bit. Now, you have some more coffee and clean up that plate...."

It was just past nine when Maggie parked her car under a box elder tree at the base of the dirt road to the mine. The road cut up the side of the mountain just behind the county works, where all the heavy machinery for Del Oro County was kept and serviced.

Carrying only a flashlight, Maggie began climbing to the accompaniment of a chainsaw's scream and the roar of a revving backhoe. She'd huffed up two cutbacks before she left the sounds of civilization behind.

The hike took over an hour. It brought a sheen of sweat to Maggie's brow and wet spots beneath the arms of her shirt. But the exertion was invigorating. She possessed an abundance of physical energy, which in Phoenix she worked off four or five times a week at her health club. Inactivity made her restless. As she neared the mine site, she realized that just getting out and working up a sweat was doing wonders for her attitude. She felt better than she had since receiving the news of Bryan's death.

The public road, crisscrossed with streams and deeply rutted from snow runoff, wound on past the place where the access road to the Hard Luck Lady cut back down the side of the mountain.

Maggie stood at the top of the steep turnoff, panting a little from her effort. The private road that fell away beneath her was free of debris. Bryan must have been up here to clear it of fallen branches and dead trees since the past winter's snow.

The optimism created by getting a little exercise began to fade. Maggie dreaded going down there.

The Hard Luck Lady was a hardrock mine—a hole in the ground, presumably allowing access to buried ledges of gold-bearing quartz rock. To Maggie, this particular hardrock mine was a bottomless pit into which all of her family's dreams and hopes had been tossed.

When her father had died, she'd begged her mother to simply let the mine go, stop performing the required yearly assessment work so the rights would revert to the government. But neither her mother nor Bryan would hear of that. The Hard Luck Lady had been Harry Durrant's dream. And though that dream had kept him from ever making enough money to take care of his family, his wife and son refused to let it die. At first Julie Durrant had hired friends to do the work each year. Later Bryan had taken over.

Now all of them were gone: Harry, Julie and Bryan. Harry had spent all of Julie's money. Bryan had lost the house. All that remained was this hole in the ground, a

blacksmith's shed beside it and the one-room shack
nearby, where her father used to stay when he was working up here.

From a few cutbacks below her on the public road,
Maggie heard the sound of a truck engine. She ignored it.
There weren't a lot of reasons someone might be on the
road, but it was a free country, after all.

Struck by the bright rays of the late-morning sun, the
corrugated iron roof of her father's shack glared at Maggie through the trees. Maggie blinked against the glare,
wiped the sweat from her brow and started down.

The access road was so steep that gravity had her at a run
in seconds. She could have dug in her heels and taken it
slower, but she didn't. Concentrating on the challenge of
keeping her feet as she fled down the hill served a purpose. It took her mind, for a few short seconds at least,
away from unhappy thoughts. She was at the bottom and
standing by the shack in no time at all.

The shack, sided in the same corrugated iron that covered the roof, had a padlock on the door. Maggie carried
the key to the lock in her pocket, but a glance in the single
dusty window told her all she needed to know. Accom-
modations in there were as primitive as she remembered.
Rough shelves lined the walls, and a wood stove stood next
to a dry sink. The stained mattress had been canted on its
side against a wall, and the empty bed frame waited
nearby.

Having seen enough, Maggie turned away toward the
mine itself. She barely glanced at the blacksmith's shed,
where her father and brother had sharpened their tools,
except to note that the door lacked a lock and was hanging halfway off its hinges.

Near her booted feet two parallel rails, like a rusted
double tongue, led down from the mine entrance. One

single ore car, its iron oxidized red from exposure to the elements, sat empty at the end of that forked tongue. Against a pile of quartz rubble, an air compressor and a squirrel-cage fan lay rusting in the sun next to a generator and a pile of six-inch pipe.

Maggie knew enough about the process of hardrock mining to know that Bryan must have been planning to install a ventilation system to pump fresh air into the mine, as well as laying water lines for drilling. He'd got as far as buying the equipment—several thousand dollars worth—and then he'd never managed to get the system in and working. He'd been lucky someone hadn't come by, loaded the whole mess on the back of a truck and driven off with it.

Maggie stepped past the idle machinery and up to the portal. Standing there at the mouth of the mine, she had moved into the shadow of the mountain into which the mine was cut. She looked into blackness. Before her lay an almost horizontal tunnel, or adit, which had been dug on a slight slant so that standing water would drain out and ore cars loaded with mineral-bearing rock would roll down and out, as well.

Maggie entered the blackness. The instant drop in temperature caused her to shiver. She felt the sweat the hike had brought out turning cold on her skin.

The smell was as she remembered, mineral and dank. She turned on her flashlight and shot the beam around. New timbers braced the wet rock walls, more evidence that Bryan had put everything he had into the mine.

Maggie shined her light up the drift, checking the floor so she could avoid the puddles of undrained water all along the tunnel. She would have to go farther in to see what else Bryan had been up to. In her father's day the tunnel had ended after one turn in less than two hundred feet. Maggie pointed her light into the blackness and started picking her way around the standing water.

She'd gone three steps when she heard the engine of a truck. Though the sound was faint, muffled by the mountain that surrounded her on three sides, there was no mistaking that the sound was coming nearer. Someone was driving down the access road. Maggie switched off her flashlight.

She heard the gears shifting as the driver turned around at the base of the road in the space behind the shack. Then there was silence. A truck door slammed. Booted feet walked around the shack, paused once or twice and then approached the tunnel.

Maggie didn't move. Not because she was afraid, but because she was hoping that if she just waited, whoever it was would go away and leave her alone to her sad business here.

But then a light flashed into the blackness and found her.

"Maggie."

She turned quickly, and the light blinded her. Maggie threw up a hand; the light was switched off. She waited for a moment to let her eyes readjust. Then she saw that a shadow blocked the cave entrance—the tall, broad shadow of a man. Maggie didn't need the evidence of her eyes, though, to know who was there. She'd known when he formed the first syllable of her name. It was Mac.

Five

Maggie slogged through the stagnant water to confront him.

"What are you doing here?" she demanded when she'd reached the entrance where he stood.

He smiled, his teeth flashing very white in the darkness. "I stopped in at the café. Odetta told me where you were headed. Thought you might like a ride."

"I walked. It was no problem."

He shrugged. "I can give you a ride back."

"If I didn't need a ride up, I certainly don't need one back down."

"That's all right. I'll take you, anyway, since I'm here."

Maggie's exasperation rose. How much clearer could she be? "I said no, thank you."

"And I said I'll wait." He turned and went out into the sun. He wore jeans and a plain white T-shirt. The T-shirt emphasized his powerful shoulders. The jeans hugged his behind.

All the longing for him that she'd been doing her best to ignore for the past day and a half flooded over her. She yearned to run after him and throw her arms around him. She hated that yearning because, in the end, it could come to nothing at all.

Out in the sun Mac turned and sat down on a boulder not far from all of Bryan's unused machinery. He squinted in Maggie's direction, shading his eyes against the sun with a forearm. "Go ahead and finish whatever it is you're doing. I'll wait right here."

Maggie's frustration impelled her out of the dark cave to where he sat so insolently on his rock. "I told you the other night, Mac. The answer is no."

He looked up at her, still shading his eyes. "I heard you. And I understand."

"Then why are you here?"

He didn't answer for a moment. He regarded her steadily from beneath the shadow of his arm. Then he stood up, swiftly enough that she fell back a step. He paced to the pile of rubble and all the rusting equipment, then he turned abruptly back to her.

He said, "Damn it, Maggie. I like you. A lot. Besides wanting you like hell. If you won't let yourself want me back, that's your business. I can respect that and learn to accept it."

"That's not what you said the other night."

"I've had a little time to... cool off since then. If you insist there can't be anything between us as a man and a woman, then that's how it'll be. In the end it takes two or it's no good. But lovers or not, I still can't stand to see you putting yourself through all this alone. Yesterday you went all over town writing out checks to pay debts that aren't even yours."

"How do you know what I did yesterday?"

"It's all over town, Maggie."

"Right." Her words were bitter in her mouth. "Just like it's always been. They've all got their noses in everyone else's business."

"It's a small town. Part of caring is wanting to know what's happening with your neighbors."

Maggie chuckled sarcastically. "Caring? It's gossip, pure and simple."

"I guess we just look at it differently." His voice was mild.

"You're right about that. And for your information, Bryan's debts *are* my debts. They're family debts. No one ever again will be able to say that the Durrants aren't paid up in Brandy City."

"What does it matter what they say? You just told me that it was only gossip, anyway. What does a bunch of gossip matter, especially when you live a thousand miles away?"

Maggie shouldn't let herself argue with him; it was none of his business, anyway. *She* knew what she was doing; what he thought didn't matter. Yet she heard her voice responding without her conscious permission. "It matters. I want it all finished. I want it done for good."

"What?"

"I just want to be paid up. Just leave it at that."

For a moment he glared at her. Then he sighed and raked his hand through his hair. "All right. You want to be paid up. Fine." He threw out an arm in a sweeping gesture that took in the rusting machinery, the mine and the iron-sided shack. "Then could you just explain what the hell you're *doing* up here all alone?"

Defensiveness moved within Maggie, as if it were a living thing, tightening her stomach, constricting her throat. "This mine is my responsibility now. I needed to see exactly what I'm responsible for."

"Why?"

"What do you mean, why? I just told you."

"It doesn't wash. You also told me you had plenty of money of your own. And when you talked about this mine the night before last, I got the impression if you never saw it again, it would be all the better for you. There's certainly no need for you to rush right up here now all by yourself."

"Yes, there is. I'm taking care of everything as soon as possible. I want everything wrapped up. This time, when I leave Brandy City, I'll never have to come back again."

He shook his head. "You should hear yourself. You sound like a kid running away from home."

"This is not my home!"

Maggie didn't realize she'd shouted the words until the awful silence that followed them.

Then she sank to the boulder Mac had been sitting on before. She looked down at the ground between her feet. She could feel Mac's gaze on her.

She said, "I just have to do this my own way, Mac."

"All right. But let me drive you down when you're through here."

She sighed. "It's only playing with dynamite, you know that. You and I—"

He cut her off. "It's a ride in a truck, that's all. I'll need both hands for the road, so your gorgeous body will be safe."

She allowed herself to look at him, shading her eyes against the glare of the sun. "Is there any way to tell you no and have it stick?"

He grinned. "Keep trying. You're bound to get through to me eventually."

A little voice in her head scolded that the real reason he wasn't believing her *no's* was that she was sending out conflicting signals. Somewhere down inside she didn't want to get rid of him at all. She wanted to trust him; she wanted to let him help her in any way he wanted to help her. She wanted him to take her to his beautiful house and she wanted to be brave enough to follow him inside. What might happen then, she dared not even contemplate.

He interrupted her dangerous reflections by gently saying her name.

"All right, I'll go back down with you," she answered, though he hadn't asked again in words. Then she added with a minimum of irony, "Since it's only a ride in a truck." She stood up. "I want to go back in the tunnel to finish looking around. And then, when I come back out, maybe you could help me get some of this equipment into the shack where it'll be out of the weather and under lock and key."

"Give me the key," he said. "I'll get started right now."

She took it from her pocket and tossed it to him. He caught it neatly. She read his smile as if he'd spoken. She was wary of getting close enough to hand him the key, and he knew it.

She wondered, her face coloring, if he was thinking of the other night, when she'd passed him the check and her fingers had brushed his. That little touch had set off a flash fire that had taken all her will to bring under control. And still the fire burned, banked but hungry to be fueled to a blaze once more.

Maggie gulped and pushed the memory of the other night away. "I'll only be a minute," she said.

He tossed the key up in the air and caught it neatly. "Take your time. I'll be here."

She turned to the tunnel entrance again, savoring those last three words of his in spite of herself.

I'll be here. What a beautiful thought.

Inside the tunnel it was every bit as dank and cold as it had been before. But to Maggie it didn't seem so bad now.

She discovered quickly that Bryan hadn't done much else beyond retimbering. There was a new raise, or vertical excavation, just around the bend before the main tunnel ended. Maggie poked her head up there and shone the light around. Her light picked up the metallic gleam right away. A ledge of heavily mineralized quartz; in such ledges gold was found. Bryan had blasted the raise to get to it.

Maggie gave a cold chuckle. She had no doubt that there was gold in the quartz ledge. The problem had never been that the Hard Luck Lady was played out. There was lots of gold in her, just as Harry Durrant had spent his life insisting. The problem was always that getting to the ore, getting it out and then milling it would cost more than the final product would be worth.

Bryan had sold their mother's house to take another shot at his father's dream. It had been a fool's dream. No paltry tens of thousands would have been enough to buy more than a few new pieces of equipment to be left to rust out in the elements.

Maggie left the dark tunnel behind. She joined Mac, who had the cabin opened and was hauling things into it. He went to his truck and brought out an extra pair of gloves for her. She thanked him and started working alongside him.

The stuff was heavy, but they were both strong. Within a half hour they had everything inside.

Before they went back down the mountain, Mac produced a couple of sodas from a cooler in the bed of his truck. The fizzy sweet stuff felt wonderful sliding down Maggie's parched throat. Maggie found herself thinking again that she was grateful he had followed her, though she knew it would be unwise to tell him so. They sat, not speaking, beneath a Jeffrey pine. In the shade the breeze cooled the sweat on her skin.

She felt better now that the wasteful evidence of Bryan's folly was safely locked in the shack. At least it wouldn't be stolen or disintegrate further before she decided what to do with it.

"Your left braid is falling down," Mac said, tipping his soda can at her. He was stretched out on an elbow on the bed of needles beneath the tree.

Maggie set her can down and raised her arms to pin the twist of hair back in place. Just as she did so, she saw a flicker of movement from behind the shack.

Maggie froze, her arms above her head. "Look, Mac." She only mouthed the words and she didn't glance his way. But she felt the force of his attention as he turned to follow the direction of her gaze.

From between the shack and Mac's truck, in a procession at once stately and fragile, came a doe and two fawns. They moved into the bright sunlight, ears twitching, wide eyes wary. When they stood in a line clear of the shack, all three of them—mother and young—turned their fine heads on their long necks at once. Three sets of black nostrils quivered as they scented the human intruders beneath the pine tree.

Both Mac and Maggie remained absolutely still. The three deer regarded them, unmoving, for the longest time. Then, with great dignity, the doe turned away. She strode proudly to the side of the road, and then surged up the high bank, causing a minor slide of dirt and rock. Her young followed her, imitating her moves almost exactly. She disappeared into the trees soon enough, the two less agile fawns just behind her.

Maggie watched after them, hardly aware that she remained sitting with upraised arms, halfway through the act of pinning up her fallen braid. Then she said, without taking her eyes from the spot where the doe had disappeared, "My father used to say that sighting twin fawns brings good fortune before sunset. I wish it were true."

"The day is young."

Maggie shot him a look, feeling suddenly foolish. He returned her gaze, his dark eyes warm. Maggie hastily repinned her braid and stood up. "We should go back. I want to get into the house today, start deciding about what to do with the things in there."

Mac stood up, too, and smashed his can to a flat cylinder on a rock. Maggie did the same to hers and then handed it over to him, careful not to let their fingers touch.

"Thank you," she said. "For the soda. For your help."

"Anytime."

Maggie thought she could lose herself in the warm darkness of his eyes, lose herself and be perfectly happy that way, never to be found. They went on looking at each other.

At last she said, "We should get back."

"Right," he said.

They turned in unison, like a pair of unwilling puppets directed by insistent strings, and went to his truck.

During the ride down the side of the mountain, neither Mac nor Maggie had much to say. Maggie told herself it was better that way. Conversation would most likely take them to subjects better left closed.

At the base of the road Mac let her off by her car. Maggie shut the door behind her and leaned in the open window to thank him one more time.

"If you need anything...*anything*," he told her, "you call me."

Maggie shook her head. "You know that wouldn't be wise."

"Then call Allison Clay. She's a friend, isn't she?"

"Yes," Maggie confessed. "Allison has always been a friend."

"Then call her. Call someone, Maggie. Don't try to deal with everything Bryan left undone, *and* your grief, all alone. Promise me, Maggie."

She promised, though she knew that calling Allison was going to be unnecessary. Her emotions weren't exactly reliable, but she was managing quite well to keep her sorrow at bay. She intended to continue that way until she'd tied up all of Bryan's loose ends. Grief wouldn't be getting hold of Maggie Durrant until long after she'd left Brandy City and Sluicer's Bar behind.

Maggie stood by her car beneath the dappled shadow of the box elder and watched Mac drive away. Regret tugged at her heart. If only...

With a sigh she left the yearning thought unfinished. She'd made her choice about Mac. Her mixed-up emotions were only lagging behind her good sense a little. Her choice was bound to be difficult to live with as long as she remained in Brandy City, where a woman couldn't have breakfast without being told how wonderful the man was.

It took no genius to see the solution to her problem. She must get things over and done with and get out as quickly as she could.

Her mother's house was next on the list. Maggie got in her car and drove straight there.

She had sense enough now not to linger outside, pondering the deterioration time had caused. Nor did she allow herself a single glimpse at the graceful house across the creek.

She emerged briskly from the car, stopped at the trunk for an armful of empty boxes and let herself through the squeaky gate. She ignored the complaining of the old boards beneath her feet on the side porch.

Once in the side door, she set her load of boxes down on the cracked linoleum. She left the door open behind her to let in a little fresh air. Then she permitted herself a moment's pause to decide where to begin the chore of packing up.

There were all the dishes and cooking utensils in the kitchen, of course. That might be a good place to start.

She looked down the long room in front of her. The bathroom, added on a few years before Maggie's birth, as well as the stairs to the second floor, lay at the end of it. Cupboards, counters, a combination wood-and-gas stove, an ancient refrigerator and the old chipped sink lined the walls.

Maggie could see from her spot by the door that the sink was piled with dirty dishes. She'd need to clean them up first before she could start packing them.

She started toward the sink.

And then it occurred to her that perhaps upstairs would be a better place to begin. She turned for the door that led to the narrow, steep stairs.

But up there was where she and Bryan used to sleep as children. She just didn't think she was ready to deal with the flood of memories the cramped rooms beneath the eaves would release.

The bathroom, then. She put her hand on the old porcelain knob. But then she pictured the full-length mirror on the other side of the door. The mirror would have a diagonal crack in it, from top left corner to bottom right. Her father had done that one night when he came home drunk.

No, Maggie didn't want to see that crack right this minute.

Maybe she'd just start in the living room.

She backtracked down the long kitchen and turned into the main living area. Beneath a front window her mother's old desk was buried in papers. Going through them would most likely mean finding more unpaid bills to take care of.

And what else might she find? Old correspondence of her mother's? An unfinished letter to herself from her brother, asking for another loan?

Just to tide me over, Maggs. Things are a little tight right now....

Maggie shook her head. She just couldn't handle seeing anything like that yet.

Seeking a start that wouldn't break down the carefully constructed floodgates of her emotions, Maggie pushed aside the flowered curtain and entered the downstairs bedroom.

The cramped room remained the same as it had been five days before. Bryan's things still littered every available surface.

Maggie decided she'd found a beginning she could handle. She went out to the kitchen for a couple of boxes and then she returned and began straightening the room.

When all was orderly again, Maggie lingered, thinking vaguely that she still hadn't put anything in the boxes; she should begin packing up.

"Soon. I'll get started soon," she whispered to herself as she lovingly stroked the rusty metal bedstead and set the creaky cane rocker to rocking.

Julie Durrant had sat in that very rocker, sixteen years before, on the day she told her daughter of the will she'd made.

"I'm leaving everything to Bryan, honey," Julie had said. "Bryan's not like you, he's just not tough. He'll never make it if I don't leave him something to start with when I go."

Staring at the empty rocker, Maggie felt again the stab of jealousy that had pierced her heart at her mother's words. Her mother had loved her, but *adored* Bryan. Maggie had always known it—and more or less accepted it. But on hearing that there would be nothing at all for her that she didn't create with her own hands, some grasping, hungry part of her had wanted to scream: Bryan won't make it, anyway! He thinks the world owes him a living. If you give him everything, he'll only lose it all!

But even at seventeen, she had known that such ranting would do no good. And beyond that, her mother was right. Maggie was bound to succeed, whether she had this dinky, dark house and the rights to a worthless gold mine or not.

She had taken her mother's hand. "It's all right, Mama. I understand," she had said. Thirteen years later, when Julie Durrant died, her will had held no surprises for her only daughter, Maggie.

Slowly the old rocker creaked to a stop. Maggie dropped to the side of the just-made bed, facing the window that looked out on a snarl of wild rosebushes.

"Take care of our Bryan," her mother had said not long before she died. "You're the strong one, Maggie. I know you've got your own life now, but do what you can. Look out for my baby."

Maggie had agreed, though inside she seethed.

Julie Foley Durrant had been of good family. She'd had everything. Money, parents who doted on her, the promise of a decent education. Before Julie fell in love with Harry Durrant, Judge Foley had planned to send his only daughter to Stanford. But she'd thrown it all away on two worthless men: her husband and later the son she bore him.

Harry Durrant had died at the age of forty-six of the miner's lung disease, silicosis, leaving Julie to support her family by working at the Gold Pan.

"There's no shame in honest work, Margaret," Julie had said proudly.

And Maggie had wanted to shout back, *Why didn't you tell that to Daddy, or how about to Bryan?*

Look out for Bryan, look out for my baby.... Maggie recalled again her mother's dying request.

And Maggie had promised she would.

In the streaked dresser mirror by the window, Maggie could see her own reflection. She quickly looked down at the hands clasped in her lap. She didn't want to look at herself, because what she saw was a woman who hadn't kept her promise.

Bryan was dead. Maggie had promised to watch out for him, and she'd done that by sending him money whenever he asked for it. Yes, she'd loved him and wanted the best for him. But she'd also despised him for being as weak as their father was, for never in his life taking responsibility for the things that he did. She lived far away and she'd given up on him. Now he was lost to her—the last of her family gone for good and all. The only relative she had left was the heartless old man who lived on Mercantile Street, and he was less than nothing to her.

With a kind of numb puzzlement, Maggie saw the first tear drop onto her clasped hands. Then she heard her own moan and felt her shoulders starting to shake.

It hurt very badly. This grief that she had been determined not to let get hold of her yet. She clutched her stomach like a woman poisoned and she tried to hold it back.

But it could not be held back. The tears came faster, flooding over the dam of her lids and streaming down her face.

"Oh, no. Oh, please, no..." she heard herself crying. The sound was animal and horrible and naked in its pain.

Trying to straighten herself, since her body seemed to be caving in on itself, she looked up. She saw herself in the mirror, her face streaming tears and contorted in grief.

And she saw Mac Manero standing behind her in the doorway.

Six

Mac held her flashlight. Some tiny corner of her mind that remained capable of rational thought understood that she must have left it in the truck.

His dark gaze took in everything at a glance—her streaming face, the blank agony in her eyes. "God, Maggie," he said.

Maggie had never felt so vulnerable in her life. She knew the fear and desperation of a wounded animal, discovered torn and bleeding in its lair.

"Go away." Her voice broke on an ugly sob. "Leave me alone."

He ignored her words. He tossed the flashlight on the old rocker, which set to creaking once again. He came toward her, dwarfing the cramped room.

"It's nothing." She told the lie on a ragged moan. "It'll pass. Please go...."

He came around the end of the bed, edging his big frame between it and the dresser. He stood right in front of her, blocking the mirror and the window.

Maggie ran out of words to send him away. She looked up at him, dumb. The tears continued to course down her cheeks.

He returned her look, his eyes steady and full of understanding. He said, "Yes. It's good. It's what you need to do."

Wordless, all of her defenses blasted to dust, Maggie reached up pleading hands to him. He took her by the waist as her arms circled his neck.

Maggie fit herself against his body, which was warm and strong and broader than her own. Then she let the racking sobs shudder through her as she buried her head in the crook of his neck, drenching the collar of his shirt.

He held her close, stroking her back and her hair, mumbling beautiful things in Spanish that her ears didn't understand. Yet her heart understood every word.

"It's all right, *mi reina*. It's good," he whispered against her hair. Then she clutched him tighter still, and a fresh onslaught of tears began.

Maggie had no idea how long they stood locked together in the small, dark room. She only knew, as the storm of tears subsided, that she felt better than she had in days. Exhausted, yes. Drained and weak. But cleansed of the crippling sorrow that had been beating at the walls of her composure since she'd learned her brother was gone.

She shifted slightly in Mac's arms. His hold on her relaxed as she lifted her head from his shoulder and slid her hands from around his neck down to his chest. They stood for a moment, her forehead against his chin.

She sniffled. Mac saw her discomfort and reached for the box of tissues on the dresser. She took one and blew her nose.

"I promised my mother I'd take care of Bryan," she said, her voice like a tenuous thread feeling its way around the constriction the flood of tears had created. "I broke my promise, and now he's gone forever."

"He was an adult, Maggie," Mac said softly. "It's not your fault that he always refused to take on the burdens of a man."

"I despised him almost as much as I loved him." She whispered the confession, looking at Mac's shoulder rather than at him. "A part of me despised *all* of them—my mother, my father *and* Bryan. The *Dreamin' Durrants,* like people always said. Too busy dreaming to get anything done. They were my family, but I hated being one of them. I couldn't wait to get out of this town—to go someplace where I wouldn't have to be one of them ever again."

Maggie sank to the bed, and Mac sat beside her.

She blew her nose again and stared out the window at the tangled rosebush. She began to speak, revealing her guilt and her pain in a soft flood of words.

"My father was so...*hopeless* as a provider. He was always just one step away from the big strike up at the Hard Luck Lady that was going to make us all rich." Maggie shook her head. "They had a hundred names for him in town. They called him Dreamin' Durrant. Or Hard Luck Harry, after the mine and because when he'd get drunk he loved to go on about all the hard luck that was keeping him from ever quite getting on top of things. Or High Gradin' Harry—you know what high grading is?"

"Tell me."

"After a really rich vein is blasted in a hardrock mine, there can be chunks of rich, high-grade ore lying around the tunnel at the blast site. When the guys who are working the mine go in and steal that ore, that's high grading. More than one miner working for someone else has done that, even though it's thievery. No one that I know of was ever actually caught at it—except my father. He got caught up at the Stoney Creek Mine trying to leave after his shift with his pockets full of high grade. He just had his head too much in the clouds to be minimally cautious.''

''Was he arrested?''

''No, they were easy on him. He was like Bryan—everybody liked him and considered him basically harmless. They took the ore back and fired him. That was fine with him, of course. He never liked working anywhere but the Hard Luck Lady, anyway. Everyone in town laughed about it for years. Dreamin' Durrant, the only guy in Del Oro County who could actually manage to get himself caught high grading….'' Maggie gave another painful laugh that ended on a sob.

She blew her nose again and went on. ''My mother adored him, though. She always believed in him. She was born *somebody* in this town. He made her into a nobody. He took everything she had except this run-down house and he left her up to her eyeballs in debt, and she went on loving him. She loved him to distraction while he was alive, and after that she loved his memory.

''She was the same about Bryan.'' Maggie looked down at her hands and the soggy tissue she held. ''I always felt cheated at the way she put Bryan over me. When Daddy died, Mama got the job at the Gold Pan. I was hired to clean rooms at Anderson's Motel. Bryan did nothing to help out. Mama said he was just a baby.''

Maggie turned and tossed the tissue in the wastebasket at the end of the dresser. ''He was always just a baby,'' she said. ''Until the day he died.''

"And you resented that?" Mac asked in a noncommittal voice.

Maggie turned to look him in the eye for the first time. "You're damned right I did."

He shrugged. "I can understand that. You're strong, Maggie. Your family took advantage of your strength. You did what you could for them, and then you got away in order to give yourself a chance for your own life. Things couldn't have gone any differently without you doing what you despised your mother for doing—sacrificing your own future for them."

Maggie looked out the window again. "Then why do I feel so *awful?*"

"You loved them. And they're all gone now. You feel regrets—what you *might* have done differently, if only you'd known." Mac took her hand. "But you *didn't* know, Maggie. And if you look at what you really could have done, it would only have been a mistake—to stay here and put aside your life for your brother's sake. What good would that have been? And could you have stopped him from getting drunk and then getting in his truck a week ago, anyway?"

"Probably not," Maggie admitted.

"Then there's nothing to do but what you *are* doing. Let yourself grieve and remember him with love, with all his faults. Remember all of them with love. They helped to shape your life, though in the end *you're* the one who made you who you are."

Mac's hand was warm around hers. Maggie squeezed it. "I know you're right," she said.

"It'll be better now." He took both her hands, tugging on them a little so she would look up into his eyes. "We need to get out of here," he said. It didn't seem odd to her that he included himself as needing to leave, too. Something had happened between them in this room; a bond had been forged. What she had shared with him made him as aware as she was of the ghosts that lingered in her mother's house.

"I've barely started packing up," she said, sparing a regretful glance at the open boxes she'd brought in and set on the dresser top. "Today I planned on getting at least a room or two cleared out."

"Is there some reason you need to get out of town fast?" His voice was half-joking. A teasing light brightened his dark eyes.

It seemed perfectly natural now to answer his question with frankness. "To tell the truth," she said, "I *was* trying to get away from you."

"I'm that threatening?" The teasing light had left his eyes. She understood that he wanted an honest answer.

"You're...different. Different than other men I've known."

"Meaning?"

"You don't give up, on any level. You're relentless as the river."

"You don't like that?"

"It scares me, I guess. And then there's the way you understand what's happening to me before I do myself. But then I suppose it's logical that you would. You lost your family, too, in a terrible way. And you learned to accept it and go on with your life."

Maggie looked down at their clasped hands and then back up at him. "I suppose what you said about me the other night was true. I have a problem with men. You're definitely a man, so no matter how much I'm drawn to you, it's not easy for me to trust you." Maggie fell silent, wondering where she'd found the courage to tell him so much.

Mac ended the silence. "Do you want to trust me?"

Her throat felt tight; she had to look away. "Yes."

Tenderly he tugged on her hand until she dared to look at him once more. "I'll tell you what *I* want."

"Okay."

"I want you to give it a shot, Maggie. Give yourself a chance at trusting me."

Maggie thought of what had just passed between them, of the way he had made himself a conduit for her pain. He had let it wash through him and away. In her entire life no one had ever done a thing like that for her.

She asked tentatively, "Give it a shot?"

"Yes."

"How?"

He looked at her for a moment and then asked, "Are you due back in Phoenix soon?"

She shook her head. "I work for myself. Or that is, I *did* work for myself. I was co-owner with another woman in a chain of video rental stores."

"You sold out?"

Maggie nodded. "We started out with one store seven years ago. We made that one into eight. I'd been ready to move on for a year or two. A few months ago my partner bought me out. Before I got the call about Bryan, I had been spending my days scouting new business opportunities."

"So you don't really have to be in a big hurry. You *could* take your time about this and not push yourself so hard."

"Well . . ."

"I mean," he said carefully, "that you could stay in Brandy City as long as you needed—as long as getting everything settled might take."

Maggie thought about that and admitted that he had a point. All the frantic rushing around hadn't succeeded in doing much beyond forcing her up against an emotional wall. She needed a little time to decide what to do about the mine. And packing up this house would be packing up her childhood. She wouldn't be able to streak through it grabbing things out of drawers and tossing them in boxes. It was going to take a while.

"Yes," she said. "I suppose taking it slower would be a wise decision."

Mac looked down at their entwined hands. Smoothing her fingers open, he kissed her palm the way he had done the other night in her motel room. Maggie felt her whole body yearning toward the caress.

"What about you and me, then?" she heard herself asking, her voice suddenly soft.

"We could take that real slow, too," he murmured against her palm. "One little step at a time. And see how it goes."

His warm breath played over her open hand. He kissed each of her fingers.

Maggie said, in a tone both husky and tart, "So far, I'm not seeing much evidence of you taking it *slow*, Mac."

Mac glanced up, a warm gleam in his eyes. Then he stood. He gave a playful tug on her hand. "Come on, woman. Let's get out of here." He pulled her toward the curtained door.

She shook her head, bewildered at his sudden change of mood. "Where are we going?"

"To my house. It's lunchtime and I'm starving." He shoved away the dusty curtain and strode across the rotting linoleum floor.

Maggie decided that she was starving, too. She allowed herself to be towed along, docile about following a man for perhaps the first time in her life.

Mac led her out through the side door, pausing just long enough to close it behind them. Then he went off the porch the back way and down the bank to the creek, never letting go of her hand.

"Mac, what's the big hurry?" She was actually giggling.

He didn't answer, just threw another "Come on" over his shoulder and forged on.

The birches and willows grew thick down in the gorge where the creek ran, so they plowed their way through them until they came to the stream.

"Isn't there an easier way to get to your house?" she asked as he began picking his way over the boulders that rose above the waterline.

"Yeah, but it's not nearly as much fun."

They jumped from rock to rock, trying not to get their boots wet and nearly making it to the far bank without mishap. But one of the rocks Mac chose had an unseen patch of wet moss on it. He hung, teetering on one foot for a moment.

"Mac, let go—" Maggie demanded, trying to yank her hand free before he took her down with him.

"Whoa!" Mac gripped her hand all the tighter, "Hold on—"

He shifted his weight, but the slippery moss gave no purchase.

"Mac!"

"Hold on—"

"Let go!"

He went down on his backside, splashing creek water and laughing as he fell.

Maggie tried to yank her hand free, but he continued to clasp it in fingers of iron. She collapsed on top of him, splashing up another cold torrent of creek water, getting her face and the front half of her body completely drenched.

"Damn you, Mac." Half kneeling and half on top of him, she punched his wet shoulder, laughing with him in spite of herself. "You could have let go."

"Never." He managed to free an arm and used it to splash more water on her with a rapid-fire movement of his hand. "I'm relentless, remember?"

"Stop that!" she sputtered beneath the barrage of cold water. "I'll get you for this...."

"Lookin' forward to it," he announced, and then grabbed her shoulders, rolling quickly and neatly so that she was underneath.

"Hey, let me up!" She bucked and wriggled and punched at his big shoulders, succeeding in getting herself entirely drenched. Then he levered himself up on his hands, still pinning her beneath the shallow current with his hips, and grinned down at her.

"Feels great, doesn't it?"

"Get off me." She tried to sound stern.

"Give me one good reason."

She thought of several: she had to strain her neck to keep her head above the rushing water; he was smashing her legs; the rocks beneath her poked into her backside; her boots needed draining. Yet not one reason seemed to matter.

In the clear space of sky between the thick trees on either bank, the noonday sun created a butter-bright halo around Mac's dark head. Maggie had to squint a little against it. And then it seemed just as easy to go ahead and close her eyes.

After what had happened in the old house, she felt an incredible lightness and an unbounded sense of freedom, as if she'd been carrying a huge weight on her back and someone—Mac, to be specific—had suddenly said, "Why don't you try putting that down?"

It was lovely, this lightness. It made it okay for her to do silly things like fall in Woodman Creek and then not get right back out again.

One of Mac's arms came behind her, supporting her. He brought her upright as he rocked back on his heels. Then he sat, lifting her neatly and settling her astride his lap. Maggie allowed all of this, smiling a tiny smile and not opening her eyes.

The water was lovely and cool, surging around their hips and gurgling in their boots. With her eyes still closed, Maggie wrapped her arms around Mac's neck.

"I think—" she began.

"Yes?" His warm breath blew deliciously over her cool, wet face.

"I think it's good to be alive, Mac."

"Yes," he said again.

Slowly, in a lovely tentative way, his lips touched hers. The water had made them cool, as cool as her own. And the coolness made them seem firmer, harder somehow. But then they warmed and softened as they opened a little, and she smiled into the warmth.

Maggie's hands went exploring. She caressed the sculpted shape of his shoulders beneath the clinging wet T-shirt. Mac nudged her lips open a little and dipped his tongue inside.

Maggie opened for him, taking his tongue into her mouth and tasting it, teasing it with her own, thinking how hot the insides of their mouths were after the coolness of their lips. He groaned a little and pulled her closer. She felt him then, rising, becoming ready for her, and she felt her own body responding, preparing the way.

"Mac..." She sighed his name into his mouth. The sound held longing as well as hesitation.

Reluctantly he pulled away. His dark eyes burned with a steady flame. Then he smiled.

Without a word he put his hands on her waist and helped her to lever herself onto her feet. Maggie stepped back. She had to struggle a little to find her balance on the slippery rocks as the racing water dragged on her ankles.

Just as she steadied herself, Mac surged to his feet before her. Water sheened off him. The wet T-shirt clung to the strong muscles of his chest and arms while his drenched jeans molded the hard curves of his thighs. He lifted his arms and slicked his hair back, wringing it of moisture with the action. The wet T-shirt was nearly transparent. She could see the shape of his pectoral muscles and the dark aureoles of masculine nipples. His big chest was nearly hairless.

Maggie wanted to put her hands on him again to trace the shape of his cool, smooth skin beneath the clinging wet shirt. She glanced up, and he caught her eye. She knew that her desire was there for him to see, betrayed by the softness of her mouth and the hunger in her eyes.

Quickly, abashed at the force of her own erotic thoughts, Maggie turned away. Mac said nothing, but began making for the opposite bank once more. He respected her reawakened wariness by not reaching for her hand.

Maggie trailed along behind him, keeping a few feet between them the whole way. Since they no longer needed to be careful of getting wet, it didn't take long to finish crossing the creek. On the other side they beat through the thick bushes again and then climbed the bank to the edge of his property.

A sandy trail lined with blackberry bushes led to a clearing rimmed with oaks and maples. Above the clearing stood the house, built flush with the driveway on the far side and mounted on stilts above the clearing from which Maggie and Mac approached. A deck dominated the west side of the house. A gust of wind came up quickly and then passed. In its wake Maggie heard the melodic tinkling of several sets of wind chimes.

Mac crossed the clearing and mounted the ramp to the deck. Maggie followed him, the water making squishing sounds in her boots. From the deck Mac opened the door to a screened porch.

He held the screen for her. She went in, boots still sloshing.

He smiled at her. "Want to get those off?"

"Yes."

The chimes she'd heard hung near the screens above their heads. There were metal ones and shell ones, and chimes made of bamboo, as well. Maggie touched one, a series of long, copper-colored pipes. It chimed rich and deep.

"They're beautiful," she said.

Mac acknowledged her compliment with a slight nod.

Mac gestured at a chair where she could take off her boots. They both bent to the task of unlacing and then took boots and socks back to the rear deck to dry in the sun.

They returned to the screened porch, where there was a door leading to the main part of the house. Mac explained that in the winter he put up storm windows and used the porch as an entry hall, a place to get in and out of coats and snow-covered boots. He led her inside.

Just as Maggie had imagined, Mac Manero's house was a place of light. The pine walls and ceilings had been left

unvarnished so that the wood retained its natural pale
color. The fireplace wall, of gray brick, added a sense of
grounding and balance. The furniture, mostly smooth,
beautifully grained eucalyptus wood, was upholstered in
nubby fabrics of blue and mauve. At this time of day the
sun pouring in the walls of windows would have bathed
everything in a blank spill of light, but Mac had the blinds
down and tipped to cup and diffuse the light as it flooded
in.

"I like everything kind of open, not a lot of separate
rooms," he said, explaining the fluidity of the space. "And
I don't really need to create extra privacy, since I live
alone." He sounded very formal, and it came to her that
he cared what she thought of his house.

She commented, "When I first saw it last week, from
outside, it made me feel peaceful. It's the same now that
I'm in it."

She knew she had pleased him. For a moment they
looked at each other. Then he said, "There's a clothes
dryer in the basement if you want to take off those wet
things."

"Do you have something I can put on?"

He thought a moment. "A robe?"

He looked so concerned and eager to be a good host that
she chuckled. "A robe would be fine."

He laughed, too. "Come on, then."

He took her through the open kitchen area to a big
bathroom complete with sunken tub, separate shower stall,
maroon towels and cedar walls. Across the way, through
an open door, she had a glimpse of what must have been
the master bedroom; another space of windows and pale
wood contrasted with an inner wall of gray brick.

"Robe's behind the door," he said. She thanked him. "I'll get changed myself," he went on, "and then fix us something to eat."

The bathroom smelled of the cedar that paneled the walls. Maggie shimmied out of her wet clothes quickly, unbraided her hair and rubbed at it briskly with a huge bath sheet. Since she was only a few inches shorter than he, Mac's maroon robe didn't dwarf her, though she had to belt it tightly to keep it from slipping off her shoulders. She faced the vanity mirror opposite the door, bent at the waist so her hair fell forward, and began combing it with her fingers.

Mac tapped on the door.

"It's open."

Maggie straightened, flipping her hair back up and over. She had a moment's glimpse of Mac in the mirror before she turned to face him. He wore a pair of black shorts and carried his wet jeans and T-shirt. She looked at his muscled legs and then forced her gaze up to meet his.

"Your clothes?" he asked.

"Oh. Yes." She bent quickly and scooped up her tangled, wet clothes. Then she felt in the pockets for her soggy wallet and her keys. "Here you go." She stood again and held out the clothes.

He took them. "There's a blow dryer in that drawer there, if you need one."

"Thanks." Maggie clutched her keys and wallet and smiled at him, thinking idiotically that she'd smiled more in the past half-hour than she normally did in a month's time.

"I'll put these in the dryer. Then I'll get lunch." He sounded as though he was reminding himself of this itinerary more than informing her. His gaze continued to take in her face, her damp hair and the way his robe had slipped slightly off of her shoulder.

"Great," she said, feeling that some kind of acknowledgment was called for, no matter how inane.

He turned for the basement door, which was tucked behind the upstairs stairwell, across from the bathroom and next to his bedroom.

"Mac?" It was out of her mouth before she realized that she had intended to speak.

He turned back to her. "What?"

She asked the question quickly. "Is there anybody you're seeing now?"

"Only you."

She smiled again at that and decided to forge on. "Have you ever been married?"

"No."

"Why not?"

He looked slightly pained. "You get right to the point, don't you?"

She answered him softly, "I like to know exactly what I'm dealing with."

"Very sensible," he said, and then was quiet. She began to wonder if he actually intended to answer her. Still holding the mound of clothes, he leaned against the little section of wall between the basement stairs and the bedroom.

Then he said, "I've lived with two women." He grinned rather devilishly. "At different times, of course."

"Of course," Maggie echoed, rolling her eyes a little.

He continued, "One, when I was in my early twenties. That lasted a little over a year. I guess you could say we grew out of each other. She was married with a baby when I left L.A." He fell silent again.

"And the other?"

He drew in a breath and shifted the soggy clothes in his arms. "That broke up when I decided to move here. Her name was Marlene, a Los Angeles woman, a lawyer, very politically active." His mouth curved in a rueful smile. "Marlene came up here twice. She said it was fine for a few days, but after a week or so the mountain stillness drove her insane." He gave a dry laugh.

Maggie asked, "What are you laughing at?"

"What Marlene said."

"And that was?"

"She told me, when we finally agreed that it just wouldn't work, that she'd tried everything to get used to it here. She said the river was driving her nuts because it would never shut up and she couldn't get to sleep at night. She said she'd tried everything, from earplugs after I went to sleep to pretending the sound was cars on a freeway. Nothing worked. She said she knew she couldn't talk me into leaving here and that she would become a raving maniac if she didn't get out of here. So that was that."

Maggie straightened the robe so that it covered her shoulder. "Do you still care for her?"

"It was more than ten years ago."

"That doesn't answer my question."

"All right. Let's say I remember her with fondness and a little regret. We were right for each other in a lot of ways. And since then I've dated, but nothing's become serious." He made a low sound in his throat. "Maybe I've grown used to being alone. Or maybe I'm too particular." He smiled again lazily, and his gaze slowly traveled from her face to her neck and then down to the V where his robe crossed over her breasts.

Maggie's skin felt warm beneath his gaze. Her senses heightened. The soft cotton robe caressed the curves and hollows of her skin. The scent of the cedar paneling sweetened the air. She glimpsed the tall windows in the bedroom beyond where Mac stood. The light that flowed in them shimmered in shifting patterns through the leaves of the trees that grew right outside. In the quiet, Maggie could hear the wind chimes on the porch, teased by the same breath of wind that moved the leaf shadows in Mac's room.

She wondered, letting her senses have their way, what it would be like to walk through the doorway to where Mac stood by the stairwell, to untie the robe she wore and let it slip off her shoulders into a maroon pool around her feet. It was an outrageous thought for someone like Maggie, who'd spent most of her life determined not to let herself get into trouble over a man.

Outrageous or not, Maggie could see herself doing it. As natural as breathing, she'd slowly approach him and then just let the robe fall. . . .

Mac's eyes burned into hers. Maggie took a hesitant step toward him.

Then she caught herself. The erotic flush on her cheeks turned to one of confusion. She looked away, toward the sunken tub along the outside wall.

Silence, ripe with unspoken desires, lay between them once more.

Mac cleared his throat. "Well, I should get these in the dryer." He went down the stairs.

Nonplussed, Maggie stared at the place where he'd been. She'd known by the smoky, lazy look in his eyes that he understood the nature of her thoughts. But when she'd turned away, he'd picked up her cue immediately and left her so that she could compose herself. This was the second time—the first being after their kiss in the creek—that he'd taken her slightest hesitation as a sign to back off.

It occurred to Maggie that his actions held a message, and a rather scary one at that. He knew that she wanted him, but he also knew she had doubts. He was holding true to his promise to take it slow—by letting her assume the lead.

He wouldn't overwhelm her as he had been willing to do two nights ago in her motel room. If Maggie wanted him, she'd have to make the first move. That was her choice, and her responsibility.

What had happened in the small, dark house across the creek had changed everything. She had never in her life trusted another human being—let alone a *man*—as she now felt she might learn to trust Mac.

They were poles apart in what each wanted of life. Never would they be able to build anything lasting. He loved Brandy City too much to ever leave it, while for her the place held too many painful memories; she couldn't live here again.

Yet there was something healing and good in what Maggie felt for Mac. The men who had shaped her life had blasted her trust. Mac, on the other hand, had shown her that all men weren't like her father or her brother or her grandfather, the judge.

Women like Maggie—strong, prickly, independent women—didn't exactly have men waiting in line. Perhaps, she told herself with a touch of irony, she'd be wise to get what she could while she had the chance.

On that note Maggie realized she'd been standing in the bathroom doorway staring blankly at the wall for minutes on end. Should Mac reappear on the stairs, she'd look foolish, to say the least. She swiftly shut the door and found the hair dryer Mac had offered.

By the time her hair fell in soft waves down her back, Maggie felt reasonably composed—if utterly unsure of what she intended to do next. One thing was certain, though. She couldn't hide in the bathroom forever. She rolled the cord around the handle of the dryer and put it away. Then she retied the belt of the oversize robe one more time. Unable to think of another reason to stall, she ventured out into the short hall.

The door to the basement was closed, which meant Mac must have come back up. She saw no sign of him in the bedroom, so she turned for the kitchen.

She found him working at the counter by the sink. The muscles played beneath the brown skin of his back as he sliced tomatoes and spread spiced mustard on dark bread.

Forgetting her apprehensions for a moment, she leaned against the wall by the refrigerator, allowing herself to appreciate the way he worked, quickly and efficiently, like a man who knows how to take care of himself and does it well.

He turned and saw her standing there.

"Cold roast beef sandwiches all right?" he asked.

"Wonderful," she told him, stepping back a little as he took the meat from the refrigerator.

He began to cut the beef in paper-thin slices with an electric knife. The meat was still pink, just the way she liked it. Mac's hands moved with authority, the slices smoothly peeling away onto the cutting board. The motor in the knife gave off a low purr.

Maggie watched Mac's hands—and accepted her own desire. She wanted those hands to touch her. Now.

"Mac?"

He thumbed the switch, and the knife fell silent.

Did he sense that she'd made a decision in the way she had asked his name? It seemed that way to Maggie, because instead of turning to look at her to find out what she wanted, he behaved as if he already knew.

He looked out the window over the sink at the locust tree there. His face, in profile to her, looked very still. He waited.

Maggie straightened from her leaning stance against the wall. Her arms, which had been crossed beneath her breasts, dropped to her sides. She covered the distance between them, her bare feet whispering on the cool tile floor.

Mac looked down at his hand on the knife. He carefully set the knife on its side, but did not turn to look at her.

Maggie said. "You were direct and honest when I asked you about the other women in your life."

He nodded and then turned slightly to rinse his hands in the sink. The running water filled up the silence for short seconds, giving Maggie a brief reprieve. Then he shut off the tap and dried his hands on a paper towel, setting it by the cutting board when he was done.

Maggie swallowed and drew in a breath. "I want you to know I've had only one lover. So I'm not very good at . . . this kind of thing. I'd probably be the only thirty-three-year-old virgin in Arizona if I hadn't started to feel like a freak when I turned thirty and gone out with one of my distributors from work. The relationship only lasted a few months. He said that he'd really been attracted to me and had wanted it to grow into something, but I was just too tense and uptight all the time. Then he stopped calling. It hurt my pride a little, I suppose. But mostly I was relieved."

Mac looked out the window, but his whole carriage was one of attention to what had been said. "Relieved in what way?"

"Well . . ." Maggie paused, considering. "I managed to get rid of my virginity without really having to learn to trust a man."

He chuckled. "I see."

They were silent. Mac still didn't look at her. He was waiting; Maggie understood that.

Boldly she reached out a hand to touch the taut skin of his back.

His body tightened beneath her hand and went still once more. "Yes, Maggie?" he asked softly.

She caressed his beautiful, smooth skin, enchanted by the sleek contours of the strong muscles beneath. "We could never have anything permanent," she said. "We want different things. I could never live in Brandy City."

"All right," he said, his voice husky and low.

Beneath the desire that was blooming in her belly and pulsing along her veins, Maggie felt hurt. He so readily agreed to her terms; he wasn't even asking, as he had the other night, for her to give it time.

But then he had told her openly that he'd grown used to being alone. He was in his late thirties. A man who had reached that age without making a major commitment probably preferred the single state.

She slid her hand up to the bulge of his shoulder and gave a gentle tug so that he turned to face her. She looked up at him. She saw desire—and restraint—in the velvet darkness of his eyes.

"We're agreed, then," she said. "This—" she sought the right word and found it "—affair will last until I return to Phoenix."

"We're agreed," he said, his tone deep and solemn.

"So much for taking it slowly." Maggie felt an ironic smile play on her lips.

"Your decision," he said, his gaze holding hers.

"Yes. I know."

Seven

Hesitantly, with her heart pounding in her ears, Maggie placed her hands on his chest. His skin was even smoother there than the skin of his back. To discover the feel of him seemed a wondrous thing. Lightly, with her palms, she rubbed. Mac sighed, and she felt his chest expand and contract beneath her touch.

She allowed her hands to roam as they wanted, sliding down to ride his trim waist and then back up again, over his chest to his shoulders. There she explored the strong cords of muscle, and then let her hands slide up his neck to the short hair at his nape. Still damp from the creek, his thick hair had a coarsely silky texture. It was heavier than her own hair, and she could feel the blunt ends as she combed it with her fingers.

She let her fingers move to his temples, where she smoothed the hair back over his ears. Then she traced the blunt line of his jaw, his square chin and the slight cleft there.

"From my father," he said of the cleft.

"Um." She touched his mouth, laying the first three fingers of her right hand lightly as butterfly wings against his lips. She felt firmness and softness and the warmth of a slowly exhaled breath.

So absorbed was she in her exploration of him that she wasn't aware he returned the favor until she felt the tension on the cord at her waist.

"Mac?" The word was tight with sudden apprehension.

"It's all right," he said. His tone soothed. "It's going to be fine."

Her arms became suddenly boneless, and her hands fell to her sides.

The cord slithered from around her waist. The loose robe parted. Maggie felt the air of the room against her skin and the new, lighter way the soft cotton draped over her breasts.

Mac's eyes looked into hers. She felt his finger, slightly rough, gently part the facings of the robe, pushing each side a little away, very slowly, until he'd bared her breasts and the front of her body. Her skin tingled and flamed where he brushed it; her nipples grew hard.

Mac continued looking only at her face. In the most secret part of herself, Maggie felt that she melted. Never in her life had she experienced anything so incredibly erotic as this man baring her body in full daylight and then continuing to look into her eyes.

Her breath came into her chest feeling thick, and it took effort to exhale, as if what she breathed had weight and sweetness, the same sweetness that was in Mac's subtle and maddening touch.

His gaze never losing hers, he pushed the robe free of her shoulders. She heard the soft weight of it hitting the cool floor.

She was totally nude.

Still he looked in her eyes.

Maggie licked her lips slowly, as they had gone dry. Her head felt as heavy as the sweet air she breathed. She longed to close her eyes, let her head fall back and wait.

For his hands.

And his lips.

And the wonder he would bring her.

"Do you want me to look at you?" His voice was so soft, it teased and it caressed. He was making an erotic game of the way their eyes held, teasing her with the moment when he would let his gaze wander downward.

"Maggie?"

She realized she hadn't answered, but she had no idea how to answer. "What?"

"Do you want me to look at all of you?"

"I . . ." No words took form.

She managed by an effort of will to hold his gaze, though her eyelids longed to droop shut in voluptuous surrender.

"Do you?" he coaxed.

Maggie gasped as she felt his touch on her nipples. He took them very gently between his thumbs and forefingers, and he rolled them.

Maggie moaned and let her head fall back. "Oh, yes," she heard herself murmur. "Yes, look at me. Look at me, Mac."

He growled low in his throat then and gathered her to him, taking her face between his cupped hands and bringing her mouth up to his.

He kissed her, his tongue tracing her lips first, and then beguiling her to part them by gently teasing her lower lip with his teeth.

Maggie surrendered again to the tender invasion of her mouth, clinging to his broad, bare chest as his tongue had its way with her. She could feel him against her hips, more ready for her than he had been at the creek. And she could feel, for her own part, that she was ready, too.

Sighing, murmuring *yes,* she let her bold hands slip downward until she felt the elastic waist of his shorts.

He groaned, and his kiss became more voracious. Maggie kissed him back, as hungry as he.

Her diligent fingers peeled the elastic waistband outward. Careful of his arousal, she slipped his shorts down over his hips. He stepped out of them and was as nude as she.

She touched him, curling her fingers around him. He ground out a passionate plea, and his breath came fast and hard into her mouth.

Then he took her shoulders and pushed her away from him, letting go of her mouth. She looked up at him, feeling dazed, thinking that never in her life had she felt this way. If this was what her father had done for her mother, no wonder her mother had let Harry Durrant take everything she had.

Mac smiled, his eyes heavy with a promise that Maggie fully intended to make sure he kept. She smiled back. Then, very slowly and deliberately, he began walking her backward.

They danced to a music only they could hear, across the cool tile, around the refrigerator, through the short hall to his bedroom, where the wide, sun-dappled bed waited. At the foot of the bed they stopped, as if their silent song had ended and they waited for another melody to see what the new rhythm would be.

They looked at each other, long and openly. Maggie thought him beautiful and told him as much. Miraculously he thought the same of her.

He touched her again as she stood before him, and the silent music that created their sensual dance began once more. He found the intimate heart of her and made love to her that way, catching her on his free arm when her legs grew weak with the pleasure he brought.

He encouraged her as he loved her, urging her to let her body find its pleasure, calling her his queen in lilting Spanish, kissing her breasts and her neck and her face until she moved in complete abandonment against his touch.

Down in the heart of her womanhood, the heat and longing built and tightened until she knew that soon it would explode outward along every nerve she possessed, a sudden spark igniting to set the world ablaze.

Though her eyes were weighted with her need, she forced them to open. "Mac, please..."

He looked up from her breasts, where his lips had been driving her ever closer to the edge. His eyes gleamed; his mouth was full and lax from kissing her.

"*¿Qué?*" he said, what?

"Please, for the first time, let it be together..." She didn't know how she got the words out, she was so intensely aroused.

"You're sure?" His husky voice coaxed her to reconsider. "It might be better, if you haven't been with a man in a while—"

Tenderly she placed her fingers on his moist lips. "It's you I want," she said. "All of you."

He smiled. "How can I refuse?"

Gently he guided her backward onto the bed. He left her for short seconds to take care of the need to protect them both. When he returned, he kissed her long and deep and touched the heart of her desire once more. She moved to his touch eagerly, fully open for him.

Then he rose above her and nudged her legs apart. She took him inside her, glorying in the feel of him filling her at last.

They moved together, as if they'd known this pleasure of each other since the dawn of time. Maggie clutched his strong back and held him ever tighter as the need and the fire built between them once more.

They moved slowly at first, savoring their joining. But then the hunger claimed them, and the rhythm became fierce and wild. Maggie felt her own explosion first, as the heat deep within her flashed out along every nerve. She cried out and clutched him ever tighter, grinding her hips against him, claiming her full pleasure as he'd urged her to do.

His fulfillment caught fire from hers, and she felt him surge ever more deeply within her, muttering her name on a low cry, tossing his head back with a deep groan.

"Yes," Maggie urged him on, and "yes," she cried again as the tremors shook them both and he strained against her cradling arms.

For a brief eternity the world was transfixed on an ever-expanding wave of white-hot delight. Then their bodies went gloriously lax in unison.

Maggie cradled him against her, stroking his moist, broad back and the taut curve of his buttocks. He moaned a little as her fingers stroked over him, sated and pleasured at once.

"Am I too heavy?"

"Shh."

He obediently fell silent. She went on stroking him, feeling the marvelous tandem slowing of their hearts.

He wasn't content for long, however, to let her do all the pleasuring. He began nuzzling her neck. Then his lips parted, and she felt the smooth stroke of his tongue. Teasingly he started to nibble her smooth skin.

"No, you don't, Mac Manero," she protested, struggling a little as she felt her body catching fire all over again. "You went and marked me the other night. There'll be no more of that."

"Wear high collars," he advised, and then bit, too softly to leave any sign.

"No way, it's the middle of summer, for heaven's sake. If I walk around in turtlenecks, I'll get overheated."

"Sounds great to me." He nuzzled some more. "I love it when you're overheated."

Giggling, she pushed him away. He gave in gracefully and rolled off of her, taking her hand.

"Come on." He rose from the bed, completely naked. The leaf shadows from beyond the windows played over the sculpted curves and angles of his big body.

Maggie looked at him, her mouth softening, thinking that what she felt when her gaze caressed him was something she'd never in her life expected to feel. It was awe at his male beauty, mingled with a warm flush of pleasure and anticipation. For as long as she remained in Brandy City, he was hers. As she was his.

For as long as she remained...

Don't you dare be sad, Maggs. It was as if she could actually hear Bryan's voice. *Have yourself a hell of a time. Love every moment of it. Life's too damned short not to grab every bit of fun you can....*

Mac was tugging on her hand. "Maggie? What is it?"

She smiled, grateful beyond measure that she could now do as Mac had suggested—think of her brother with love. "Just thinking about Bryan. Appreciating his good points. He *did* take life as it comes." Maggie left the bittersweet thoughts of her brother behind as she rose from the bed. "Okay, what next?"

Mac paused for a moment, watching her, a tender look in his eyes. She knew he'd sensed her sadness and that he wondered at its cause. But he didn't ask.

He said, "A quick shower. Together. Then lunch."

The quick shower, somehow, took forever. Mac had to thoroughly shampoo every inch of her, and then Maggie felt obliged to return the favor. Then Mac was generous enough to show her just how much passionate pleasure can be attained upright in a shower stall. Maggie found the demonstration extremely enlightening, especially right after he'd driven her to the edge of ecstasy by kneeling before her and doing things that she'd always sworn were too intimate to excite a woman like her. As she teetered on the brink, he slid upwards, taking her by the hips and guiding her long legs to wrap and cling around him. She tumbled over the edge in a sensual free-fall. He whispered heated encouragement in her ear as the steamy water pounded them, and Maggie felt the slick tile of the stall against her back.

Mac dried her very tenderly afterwards, and then they returned to the kitchen, where his robe and shorts lay in a tangle by the sink. With lithe ease he slipped into the shorts and then shook out the robe for her.

"Now, sit," he told her. "And I'll see about those sandwiches."

Maggie climbed on a stool behind the peninsula of counter that marked off the kitchen from the main living area. He finished making the sandwiches.

Maggie watched him for a moment, feeling content, grinning a little like the cat that got the cream. Then she thought about how great a big glass of milk would taste with the sandwich, and she slid off the stool to get one. Mac asked for one, too, and pointed to the pantry cabinets built against the stairs where she could find potato chips and a jar of pickles. Humming softly to herself, Maggie began setting the places for their lunch.

Out of the corner of his eye, Mac watched Maggie as she found the place mats and napkins. Her damp hair curled heavy and loose around her face, and more than once, the oversize robe she wore obligingly parted to reveal the soft curve of a breast. Once, she looked over and saw him watching. She smiled, her eyes warm and full of promise.

Mac felt like someone had hit him in the chest with a two-by-four. Less than a week had passed since their first meeting on the steps of the shabby house across the creek. Never could he have imagined then that today she would come to him and lay her soft hands on him and offer all of herself, in utter abandonment, to his hungry touch.

Mac turned away from the counter and toward her, holding the plates with the sandwiches on them.

Maggie slid onto her stool again. "All ready," she announced, gesturing at their side-by-side place mats and tall glasses of milk.

Mac came around behind her and sat on the far stool, setting her sandwich before her as he went by. They both dug in eagerly, munching potato chips between hefty bites of roast beef.

It all seemed so incredibly *right,* he kept thinking. Making love with Maggie until both of them were utterly sated, and then making lunch together, eating side by side. When they were finished, he'd check his messages. Mrs. Herrara, who rented a house he owned up Sluicer's Creek

Road, had been complaining about her water pump. He would call her and decide if he was going to have to spring for a new one. Maybe he'd take Maggie up to the house on Veneration Hill and show her the progress Lucius Clay was making remodeling it, or they could outline together a plan for clearing out her mother's house and kick around suggestions for what to do about the gold mine.

He had a feeling that from now on the subject of the mine, as well as that of the house, would not be so charged with overwhelming emotions for her.

He was still worried about her grandfather, though. She'd so completely cut the old man from her life. Mac needed to find an opportunity to tell her what he knew about that situation, and to urge her to at least visit the big house on Mercantile Street before she left town for good.

Maggie, totally unaware that Mac was plotting her reconciliation with the man she most hated in the world, picked up her napkin and dabbed at the corner of his mouth. "Mustard," she said.

"Thank you." Mac leaned across and kissed the milk mustache on her full lips. Her brown eyes shone, eager and full of life.

To love her would take no effort at all, he found himself thinking. To love her would be as natural as drawing breath.

Nothing lasts forever, a voice in his mind said. She lived in Phoenix, and he lived here. That was the given. They had both agreed that wasn't going to change. Within a few weeks her business here would be done. She would be leaving, and he'd be on his own once more.

"Why suddenly so serious?" Maggie was asking him.

"Thinking," he said.

"About what?"

He gave her a slow smile and put concerns about the future away. "How we could clear out the old house together, and about what to do with your gold mine. And if you just lean over a little bit more, I can see right down the front of that robe—not necessarily in that order."

Maggie leaned over. "Better?"

"Much."

"And now, as far as the house goes—" she began.

"What house?" He hooked a finger in the facing of the robe, so that it tented away from the soft swell of her breast even farther.

"Mac Manero, we can't spend all our time making love."

He slid his hand beneath the damp fall of her hair, cupping her head, and brought her face close to his. "No, but we can give it a hell of a try. Move your things from the motel. Today. Stay here with me."

"People will talk," she sighed.

He wanted to tell her to hell with people. But beyond desiring her as he'd never desired another woman, he *liked* her so much that he didn't want her to do anything she might regret. "I suppose you're right," he breathed resignedly.

She chuckled, her mouth so close that he shared her breath. "But what do I care what people say? I don't live here anymore. What I do is my business."

Mac pulled away a little. "Are you sure, Maggie?"

She wrapped her arms around his neck and brought his mouth right back to hers. "Absolutely. I'll drive into town and get my things—as soon as you finish what you started."

Her tender sigh as her lips pressed against his set all his senses ablaze once again. Mac surrendered to desire.

Nothing lasted forever. Mac intended to make the most of every second for as long as she was his.

Eight

Later Maggie drove into town and paid her bill at the motel while Mac went over to the house he rented to Mrs. Herrara to check on the failing water pump. Both returned to Mac's in time for a late-afternoon swim in the river.

That night they barbecued on the back deck and ate inside rather than battle the insects that always appeared around twilight. Over after-dinner liqueurs, Mac suggested she could advertise to sell the rights to the mine.

Maggie snickered in disbelief at that suggestion. "Right. And if anybody's fool enough to go for it, I'll throw in the Brooklyn Bridge for free."

"You'd be surprised," Mac said. "There's a lot of glamour in the idea of a gold mine. Owning one might appeal to someone with a little extra money to burn. You wouldn't necessarily have to make it look like anything more than it is. I'm sure a reasonably clever accountant could turn the Hard Luck Lady into a neat little tax write-off.'' Mac sipped from his glass and then added, ''The Hard Luck Lady is yours now, Maggie. You finally have your chance to get rid of it.''

Maggie thought about that. Then she said in a puzzled tone, ''I know. And I don't think I can bring myself to do it.''

''Then what?''

''I don't know.'' Maggie pushed back her chair and went to the middle of the room. She looked out one of the big windows, past the clearing to the run-down house on the other side of the creek.

Mac came to stand behind her. He put his hands on her shoulders comfortingly, and she leaned back into the solid strength of his body.

''Lord, I hated that gold mine,'' she said quietly, ''but the Lady is all I have left of them now.'' She snuggled closer against Mac, and he slid his hands around her waist.

''Do you want the house back?'' Mac asked gently in her ear, following the direction of her gaze.

Maggie shook her head. ''No. As you said, it's in terrible shape, and to fix it would amount to rebuilding from the ground up. Much better to just let it go. I've accepted that, I honestly have.'' She turned her head against the soft fabric of the maroon sweater he wore and looked at him. ''Everything starts with the Hard Luck Lady. In a way, I wouldn't be here if it weren't for that mine.''

He kissed her nose, which was tipped up to him. ''How so?''

Maggie turned to look back out the window and then began to speak. It both surprised and pleased her that talking about the past now seemed to have lost much of its power to cause her pain.

"My father got to know my mother while he was hood-winking my grandfather into investing in the mine," she said. "He charmed the wallet right out of Judge Foley's pocket at the same time as he charmed his way into Julie Foley's bed. About the time my grandfather realized he'd been had, he learned that his daughter was pregnant. He immediately disowned her—along with the fruits of her betrayal—me.

"My father married her, of course, and he always swore he'd pay the judge back as soon as he hit that major strike. He never would admit that what he'd done to the judge, inventing production reports, producing ore specimens that weren't from the Lady at all, was crooked. He died claiming that one day the Lady would pay, and Elijah Foley would get his investment back with interest."

Maggie chuckled, a wry sound. "But the Lady never paid, and Judge Foley will go to his grave cursing the name Durrant."

"I doubt that very much," Mac said.

Maggie turned to look at him again. "What do you mean?"

His black eyes were kind. "Your grandfather doesn't curse your name. I'm sure of it."

"How so?"

"Bryan told me."

Maggie peeled his arms from around her waist and stepped away, turning to face him. "I don't understand. What did Bryan say?"

"That your grandfather wanted to make amends for the past."

"I don't believe you—" Hearing the indignation in her own voice, Maggie cut herself off. She then asked cautiously, "When did Bryan tell you that?"

"Over a year ago."

"Why? I mean, why would he tell *you?*"

"Because he wanted to sign over a couple of checks your grandfather had written to him."

"You mean to pay his rent? My grandfather gave him money, and he gave it to you for rent?"

Mac nodded. "Bryan claimed he was a little short of cash at the time, and that he was too busy up at the mine to drive down to Grass Valley and deposit the checks. So I took them."

Maggie felt her nails digging into her palms and realized her fists were clenched. She ordered them to relax. "How much did the judge give him?"

Mac shook his head. "Maggie. Stop it."

"Stop what?" She whirled and moved closer to the window. She wrapped her arms around her stomach and gazed blindly out.

"Stop torturing yourself over other people's behavior. Bryan was Bryan. He's gone now. Let it be."

"How much did he take from that old man?" she demanded again, all her earlier feelings of acceptance gone.

"How would I know? He signed over a few hundred to me, and that was all I had to do with it." He took a step toward her. She whirled, and glared at him. "Maggie. Let it go."

Maggie looked at him and saw the kindness and caring in his eyes. Her anger and stubborn pride fell away. She sank to the couch in front of the window. "You're right. It doesn't matter. If Elijah Foley was fool enough to be taken in by the Durrants twice, that's his problem."

Mac shook his head. "Actually," he muttered wryly, "I was referring to letting the issue of the money go, not writing your grandfather off."

Maggie peered at him narrowly. "What are you saying?"

"That he's old and alone and he made mistakes. That you might consider the virtues of forgiveness while he's still alive, when it would mean the most."

Maggie felt very tired suddenly. She sighed and then softly spoke. "I'm not saying you're wrong. I'm just saying it isn't in me to forgive him."

"Why?"

"He disowned my mother—isn't that enough?"

"Is that everything?" His smile was tender.

Maggie threw up her hands. "Oh, all right. He disowned my mother, and he used to turn and walk away whenever he saw any of us on the street. And when my father died..." Maggie paused, unsure if she wanted to tell the rest.

Mac didn't let her off the hook. "When your father died..."

"I...I went to him. I went up to his door and I knocked on it, and when he answered I told him that Mama was crazy with grief and we were out of credit at the grocery store. I said if he would just please help us, I swore I'd pay him back someday. He looked over my head. He said, *The word of a Durrant is a worthless thing,* and he shut the door in my face."

For a time there was silence in the spacious room. Mac returned to the dining table to finish his liqueur. Then he asked, "Is that all?"

"Isn't that enough?"

He chuckled and set the small glass aside. "Yeah, I guess so."

Maggie stood up. "I can't forgive him, Mac," she said in a tone of finality. "I saw at the funeral how he is now, and maybe I sensed that he wants some kind of reconciliation with me. But I can't give it to him. He cut me and mine out of his life in a ruthless and brutal way. I can't just go to him now and give him a hug and say all is forgiven. Because it's not forgiven, and I would be lying to say otherwise, no matter how much he might need to hear that."

Mac said, "Maybe you need to say it as much as he needs to hear it."

"Not if it's a lie."

"Maggie—"

She stopped him with an upraised hand. "No more, Mac. I've had enough."

He looked at her searchingly for a moment, and Maggie steeled herself for further argument. But then he shrugged. "It's your life."

Relieved, she smiled. "Thank you for realizing that." Her voice was light. She wanted to communicate gently that, while she did appreciate all he'd done for her, any actions she took had to come by her own choice.

"I only want to help, Maggie."

"I know." She slowly approached him. "And you are." She put her arms on his chest and then slid them up to twine around his neck.

His eyes changed from piercing obsidian to black velvet. He lowered his mouth a little, and she thought he would kiss her. But then he said, his lips a breath away from hers, "Seducing me is not going to make this problem go away."

She planted a quick kiss on his chin. "As you're always telling me, Mac Manero—let it go." She started to release her arms from around his neck.

"Where do you think you're going?" He caught her arms and guided them back up where they had been.

"You mean it's all right if I seduce you after all?" she asked, feigning innocence.

His arms came around her. "Let me show you . . ."

"What?"

"Just how *all right* it is . . ."

The next morning Mac drove to Grass Valley to choose a new water pump, and Maggie braved the upstairs of her mother's house.

"Do you want me to stay and help?" Mac asked before leaving. "Mrs. Herrara can wait one more day, if you need me."

His thoughtfulness touched her. She knew he wasn't worried about the job itself, but that she might not yet be up to the task emotionally.

"I can handle it," she told him, and meant it.

He kissed her, his strong arms holding her tightly. Maggie wished he might go on kissing her forever. But life didn't run on kisses alone.

She giggled and playfully pushed him away. "Enough, or poor Mrs. Herrara *will* have to wait another day. I'll drag you back to the bedroom and lock the door behind us."

He pulled her up against his chest again. "I surrender. Take me to my room."

She peeled his hands away, stepped back and pulled open the door to his truck. "Get in. Get lost. I've got work to do."

He climbed into the truck. After he'd started the engine, he leaned out the window. "I'll be back after lunch, and I'll be ready to help you then."

She kissed him once more, quickly. "Go."

After he drove away, she took her rental car, which was still piled with boxes, down to her mother's house. She unloaded the boxes onto the side porch and marched inside, down the long kitchen and up the narrow stairs.

It amazed her how much junk could have collected it-self beneath the eaves and in the beat-up old bureaus. But she made herself be ruthless, dividing things into piles: things to keep, things to sell, things to give away and things to truck to the dump. The pile for the dump was by far the largest.

After lunch, as he'd promised, Mac joined her. The job went faster with the two of them working together. By evening they'd made a good start on the upstairs.

At twilight they swam together in a secret spot Maggie remembered from years before. They splashed and laughed like children. Maggie treasured the pure physical joy of it, feeling the cool water slide over her tired body, anticipat-ing the night to come when Mac would take her in his arms and make sweet love to her in the darkness of his room.

The next two days, Thursday and Friday, went much the same. Slowly, with Mac helping when he didn't have his own business to attend to, Maggie finished clearing out the upstairs. At Mac's suggestion, she'd posted notices all over town to the effect that there was furniture as well as odds and ends for sale from nine to five at the old Durrant place. People began dropping in to bargain or just to talk while Maggie and Mac packed.

On Thursday, Allison appeared.

"My house, for dinner, tonight." Allison extended the invitation in a tone that said, *don't argue.*

Maggie and Mac arrived at Allison's big two-story house on North Main before six. The house fairly overflowed with Clays. There were Caleb and Allison and Caleb's mother, Rose, not to mention four children, two dogs and various cats.

Dinner, barbecued ribs in Caleb's special sauce, was enjoyed outside on the big deck overlooking the river. Cal

Jr. shot off a few firecrackers beneath the deck, and Allison had to tell the sheriff when he called that it wouldn't happen again.

Caleb, whose own father had been a miner, asked about the Hard Luck Lady and offered to perform the annual assessment work for Maggie.

"I don't know, Caleb," Maggie told her friend's husband. "I haven't decided what I'll do with it yet."

Caleb smiled his shy smile. "The offer stands—just let me know."

Maggie thanked him.

Before Maggie and Mac left around eleven, Allison sold them tickets to Saturday's pancake breakfast, a fund-raiser put on by the Methodist Women in the Brandy City town hall. Maggie promised that she and Mac would attend.

They returned to the house on the hill, where Mac undressed her very slowly, kissing every inch of her, rousing her senses to a white-hot, fever pitch. Afterward they slept, all wrapped up in each other as they had been the night before and the night before that.

Well before dawn, Maggie woke. She was lying on her back, and Mac lay tight against her with one leg thrown across hers and his hand cupping a breast. For several moments she remained still, listening to his even breathing, gazing at his dark head against the white pillow.

Then, very carefully she slid out of his arms. Nude as the day she was born, she crept to the short hall, through the kitchen and out to the big, open living room. She sat backward on the couch in front of one of the huge windows, leaned her arms on the backrest, and gazed out across the dark trees that rimmed the creek to the old house on the other side. In recent years streetlights had been installed along the road, so even though the moon was down, her mother's house could be seen.

But Maggie wasn't really looking at the house. She was thinking of the night that had just passed. Of her friend, Allison, and the happiness Allison shared with Caleb and their family and all those dogs and cats.

Once during the evening, when everyone was out on the deck at the table devouring the fantastic spareribs, Allison had gone inside to plug in the coffeepot for later. Though Maggie hadn't noticed him leave, Caleb must have followed his wife. Shortly thereafter the butter dish turned up empty. Maggie had ordered Grandma Rose to stay put and gone inside to get more.

Maggie saw her friend at the sink. Caleb stood behind his wife, both arms wrapped around her waist, nuzzling her neck. Allison giggled, a sound both playful and intimate, and then she turned in Caleb's arms to receive his kiss.

Maggie had paused, frozen for a moment, just inside the glass door. An ache welled up inside her, a new yearning that she'd never in her life thought to feel. She yearned for the kind of belonging that these two married lovers knew. She wanted to belong with Mac that way, each to the other, for the rest of the time God gave them on earth.

Then Allison saw Maggie and smiled. She kissed Caleb once more, a quick, sweet peck, and then she slid out of the circle of her husband's arms. Allison asked what she could get for Maggie. Maggie held out the empty butter dish. The moment passed.

"Maggie?" Mac's sleep-roughened voice called to her from the other side of the dark room.

Maggie turned her head to see him, a shadow by the stairs. He moved then, coming into the slight radiance that fell in the windows from the thick blanket of stars above the trees. She thought that he was beautiful, hers to keep or not, standing there on the pale wood floor, completely nude and bathed in star glow. She smiled at him, though she didn't know if he could see the welcoming curve of her mouth in the darkness.

"Something wrong?" he asked.

"No, nothing." She held out her hand. He covered the remaining distance between them and pulled her up against him, threading his hands in her hair.

"The bed seems empty without you." He cupped her face and then claimed her mouth with his own.

Maggie opened herself to the enchantment his touch could bring. The voice in her heart that yearned for forever fell silent beneath the consuming flame of ephemeral desire.

Friday, while Mac was up at his Veneration Hill house going over a change in the plans with Lucius Clay, Odetta Lafray dropped in on Maggie.

As usual, Odetta got right to the point. "Heard you and Mac have gone and set up housekeeping together—how much is this rocker? I always loved the old thing."

Oddly enough, Maggie wasn't offended. She'd always known Odetta meant well, and now that she'd made some peace with the memory of her family, she found Odetta's intrusive chatter more amusing than anything else.

"For you, Odetta, that rocker is free—and yes, I'm staying up at Mac's. Does that shock you?"

Odetta waved a skinny hand in front of her face. "Heck, no. What do you think, I was born yesterday? You young people can be pretty amusing, if you want the truth." Odetta lowered her voice to a confidential whisper. "I tell you, there's nothing going on these days that we didn't do way back when—we just made less noise about it. You hear what I'm saying?"

Maggie couldn't help laughing.

"Well, I'll be," Odetta said. "I do believe that's the first time I heard you laugh since you were ankle high to a June bug. Whatever you and Mac are doing up on that hill, I think you should just keep right on doing it— You're sure about this rocker, now?"

"Absolutely."

"No, I've got to give you something for it."

"How about a free hamburger, the next time I'm by the Gold Pan?"

"It's a deal—and sweetie . . ."

"Yes?"

"I know that man's crazy about you. I'll keep working on him. We'll get a ring on that finger of yours yet."

"Odetta."

"Don't give me that mean look, Maggie Durrant. You been giving me that look for twenty years, and it never did a bit of good."

"Mac and I are not getting married."

"Never say never. It's going to be some celebration, that day. The whole town's looking forward to it."

"Then they'll be disappointed. I'm returning to Phoenix as soon as I wrap things up here."

Ignoring Maggie's protests, Odetta blithely went on. "I just want you to tie the knot within a reasonable time. Because, like I said, Andy and me are heading south before long."

"Right. You're going to sell out to Mac."

"You got it."

Maggie closed the lid on a box of pots and pans and asked, "Just out of curiosity, how much do you want for the place?"

Suddenly Odetta looked crafty. "You're interested."

"Of course not," Maggie replied too quickly. "What in the world would I do with a coffee shop in a town where I don't even live?"

"You tell me," Odetta suggested, looking irritatingly smug.

Maggie shrugged. It was silly to even inquire about Odetta's asking price. But the idea had suddenly occurred to Maggie that what Brandy City lacked was a full-sized clothing-and-notions store. People drove to Reno or Grass Valley or even to Sacramento to buy most of their clothes. Maggie had a feeling, given the convenience and reasonable prices, that a miniature "department" store would do just fine there. Also, there was the summer tourist trade to consider. That would bolster the business considerably. If a new owner were to knock out a few walls and use the massive storage room in back that now lay idle, then the Gold Pan would provide just about enough space.

"How many square feet do you have, all together?" Maggie heard herself asking.

Grinning, Odetta told her. Then she added, "You make me a reasonable offer, Maggie, and the place is yours."

"Just curiosity, Odetta," Maggie said, pushing the outlandish idea from her mind.

Along with the rocker, Odetta took two folding cots that had been stored upstairs. Maggie helped the older woman load the furniture into the back of her pickup. Mac drove up just as Odetta was climbing in behind the wheel.

Maggie gritted her teeth and waited for Odetta to start babbling about wedding rings and bridal veils. But Odetta must have decided to leave well enough alone for the time being, because she merely waved at Mac and went on her way.

That evening Mac and Maggie drove up toward Del Oro City and had dinner at Arlington's Resort a few miles outside of town. Feeling naughty and playful, Maggie told Mac she had a local landmark to show him. She instructed him to turn off on a side road halfway back to Brandy City. They bumped over a rutted dirt path for several hundred yards, and then Mac's headlights shone on an open space with a ring of rocks in the center.

"So what's the significance of this?" Mac asked. "Looks like just another deserted campsite to me."

Maggie reached over and turned the key in the ignition. The truck's engine faded into silence. "Not just *any* deserted campsite," she told him. "I'll have you know that, when I was a kid, this was one of the *major* hot necking spots of the area."

Mac's white teeth flashed in the darkness. "Necking?" he asked, as if she were speaking a foreign language. *"Necking?"*

"Yes," she informed him in a prim voice. "Necking. That's heavy-duty kissing and hugging, but mostly from the neck up."

"I know what it means," he told her. "People neck in L.A., too. I just hadn't heard the word in about a hundred years."

Maggie laughed. "I suppose you have a point. Necking is the most fun when you're panicked that your mother might find out you did it. Once you're grown up and on your own, kissing and hugging loses the glamour of being forbidden."

Their eyes had begun to adjust to the darkness. The moon, nearing fullness, shone down on the windshield through the tall pine trees.

Mac slowly ran a finger beneath the shoulder hem of her sleeveless dress. Maggie sighed and let her head drop back against the seat. "Did you do a lot of *necking* here?" Mac asked softly.

"Me?" Maggie shook her head. "Never. I wasn't going to go getting myself in trouble with any boy, that was for sure—but Caleb and Allison used to come here all the time. In fact, there is some suspicion that Cal Jr. got his start here."

"You don't say." Mac kept softly caressing her shoulder, tracing the line where her dress ended.

"It's a fact." Maggie grabbed the knit collar of his sport shirt, bringing his face close to hers. "But don't you dare tell a soul. I won't have my best friend's reputation ruined by idle gossip."

"My lips are sealed."

"Good," Maggie said, playing tough. Then she lowered her voice. "Tell me . . ."

"Yes?"

"Have you ever—" she rolled her eyes "—in a car?"

His eyelids lowered a little, and she knew he was looking at her mouth. "Maybe."

"Come on. Tell," she demanded, fisting his collar and bringing their noses close enough to touch.

"Modesty forbids," he said.

"Well, how about in a truck?" She nibbled his upper lip, just a little.

He muttered something in Spanish and tried to claim her mouth, but she held back.

"Would you like to?" she asked softly.

"¿Ahora?" he asked, now? His voice had taken on that husky thickness that she knew and loved so well.

"Yes, now."

"It might be a little awkward," he warned. He'd started doing magical things to her ear.

"But you're experienced," she said.

"Well, I'm no pro at it, if that's what you're implying."

"Don't get defensive." She nuzzled his neck. "I just wanted to know if you were qualified, is all."

Now he was the one to pull away. "*Qualified?* For what?"

"To help me relive one of the great moments of adolescence that I never got to live in the first place."

"And if I wasn't?"

"If you weren't what?"

"Qualified to help you."

"Well, aren't you?" Her tone was playful.

But Mac seemed guarded. "I didn't have a very average adolescence myself, Maggie. I was too busy working to make love to girls in cars." He pulled away a little. "I was never a run-around, Maggie."

Maggie peered at his face through the darkness. "What is it, Mac? What did I say?"

"It's . . . assumptions. I hate the damned things."

"What assumptions?"

Suddenly he was looking out his side window. "Let's forget it."

"No," she said quietly. "Let's not." She took his chin and turned his face so he was looking at her. "What assumptions?"

"Maggie—"

"Come on. Tell me."

"Oh, all right. Assumptions that I'm some kind of Latin lover or something just because I'm single and like it that way."

I'm single and like it that way. . . . The words echoed in Maggie's brain for a moment, then she ordered them to be silent. He was saying nothing that she hadn't already known. She'd seen Caleb and Allison together and felt a longing for more than what she and Mac had; that didn't mean Mac would feel the same way.

Maggie looked at him sideways and considered asking if Odetta had been giving him a bad time about his bachelor state. But then she changed her mind. Better to let it go, she thought. She wasn't responsible for Odetta's behavior, only her own.

She said, "I was only teasing. I apologize if you thought I was categorizing you."

She saw the white flash of his teeth then. He looked a little abashed. "Maybe I'm overly sensitive on the subject."

"Only you can decide about that," she said.

"You're becoming a bona fide diplomat."

"I've had a good teacher." She kissed his jaw and then whispered in his ear. "So, where were we?"

He laughed. "You just learned I lack the hands-on experience to help you relive—how did you put it?"

"One of the great moments of adolescence."

"Right."

Maggie traced little curlicues down the front of his shirt with her index finger. "Well, since neither of us is qualified, I guess we're left with only one option." Her straying finger found the waistband of his slacks.

"What?" His voice had grown husky again.

"We'll have to fake it. Together."

He said her name then, softly. And his lips met hers.

Maggie thought, as Mac's arms closed around her, that their silly banter held more truth than either of them was willing to admit. They were a man and a woman, each used to life on their own. Each at least a little bit scared of the attraction that drew them. Doing their best. Faking it together. Perhaps, she thought wistfully, they were no different than Caleb and Allison had been when they made love in this very spot more than a decade ago.

Then, after a while, Maggie didn't think at all.

* * *

The next day was the Methodist Women's pancake breakfast. Mac and Maggie arrived around nine. They sat with the Clays at one of the long tables that had been set up downstairs in the town hall. They had pancakes and sausage and drank more coffee than they should have, and held hands under the table like the adolescents they'd pretended to be the night before. When they were nearly done, Maggie excused herself to visit the rest room.

She had reached the big double doors out to the lobby and was just about to go through them when Allison called something to her from back at the table. Maggie kept going but turned her head, asking, "What?"

At that moment someone came around the door from the other side.

"Watch it!" a voice from Maggie's nightmares commanded.

Maggie collided with her grandfather. Young and stable on her feet, Maggie didn't go down. But the old man did.

Maggie reached out quickly but awkwardly to break his fall.

"No! Don't!" he said, and hit out sharply with his cane.

Maggie jumped away, clutching her arm where he'd struck her. A little wordless cry escaped her.

All brittle limbs and frail flesh, Elijah Foley hit the floor. For several interminable seconds after that, the whole crowded room was still.

Tears scalded Maggie's eyes as she looked down at the gray-faced old man. Her arm burned where he'd hit her. She felt as if she were ten years old again, shamed by her own blood before the whole town.

Maggie squeezed her eyes shut, cutting off the tears. *I am not a child,* she told herself firmly. *This mean old man's efforts to humiliate me no longer have any power over me....* The tears receded, but still her heart twisted in her chest.

Then Elijah said something she could hardly believe. "My God, Margaret. I'm sorry." He was puffing a little, clutching his side. "I'm not as steady on my feet as I used to be. I was surprised. I didn't think."

Maggie didn't know what to do. She just stared down at him dumbly, holding her stinging arm. Mac appeared like magic, as he always seemed to do in times like this.

"Stay still, Judge," he said, kneeling beside Elijah. "We'll get Fritz Laird right over here to see if anything's broken." Fritz was the nurse-practitioner who ran the local medical clinic. With a look Mac signaled Netty Beach, who picked up the phone on the wall.

"If I need Fritz Laird, I'll call him myself," the judge said flatly. The old man shot Netty Beach a look of his own, and Netty put the phone back on the hook. "There's nothing wrong with me that watching where I'm going won't fix. Now give me a hand up, will you, young man?"

Mac looked as if he wanted to argue, but then he acquiesced. Elijah rose stiffly, holding on to Mac. When he was up, he straightened his fine old suit, smoothing the collar and tugging on the points of his vest. Then he stood clear of Mac's support and leaned on his cane once more.

Maggie was still standing there, cradling her arm, feeling as she'd felt as a child in dreams when a monster rose before her and she realized that somehow her feet had been glued to the floor.

"I *am* sorry, Margaret," the judge said again. His eyes, blue as her mother's had been, seemed to plead for her understanding.

Maggie stared at him, longing to lash out at him for all the hurts throughout all the years and to run crying from the room at the same time. Then she felt Mac's touch on her arm.

Gently he rubbed the welt where the cane had struck her and then slid his hand down to twine his fingers with hers. He lifted her hand and kissed it lightly. Maggie was able to quit looking at the judge and look at Mac. He smiled at her. She forced a smile back. "I think you'll live," Mac said softly.

Something in the steady warmth of his gaze gave her strength. She turned back to her grandfather.

"It was an accident, that's all," she said, pleased at how normal she sounded. "I should have been looking where I was going."

Those blue eyes, so eerily like her mother's, still seemed to be pleading. But that didn't make any sense. Judge Elijah Foley never begged anyone for anything.

"Margaret, I'd like to—" the judge began.

"I was just on my way to the rest room," Maggie cut him off. She couldn't bear to hear more. She didn't care what he'd like to do. Just looking at him reminded her of all the bad times, when he'd snub her in the street or leave the grocery store if she or any of her family entered it.

"Excuse me, please," she murmured a little frantically, pulling her fingers free of Mac's hold and dipping to scoop up her purse, which had dropped to the floor during the collision.

"Oh, certainly, of course," said the judge as Maggie fled into the lobby.

The rest room, thank heaven, was empty. She stayed in there much longer than she needed to. She took her time, rinsing her face and hands, touching up her makeup, collecting her shattered nerves.

When she ventured back out, Elijah Foley had taken a seat two tables down from where she and Mac sat with the

Clays. For the short time they remained in the hall, Maggie did her best to pretend that the old man who had disowned her mother wasn't even there.

She expected criticism from Mac about the way she'd virtually turned and run from the old man's attempts at civility. But Mac was quiet on the return drive to Sluicer's Bar. She began to suspect that he was holding back, pondering what he was going to say to her about Elijah.

His pondering an approach was even worse than if he just hit her with it right up front. If he thought it serious enough to ponder, then that meant that, born politician that he was, it was going to be tough arguing with him once he laid it on the line.

Maggie didn't want to argue with him, not about Judge Elijah Foley. She only wanted to forget that old man and everything he stood for in her sad childhood. She'd made peace with her past. It was all behind her now. Dredging things up with the judge would only make new problems where the old ones had been solved.

When they reached Mac's house, there was a message on his machine from one of his renters, Louanne McDuffy, who lived alone in a small, somewhat isolated cabin a few miles out of Del Oro City.

"It's the pipe in the bathroom sink, Mac. It's burst and there's water *everywhere*...." On the tape Louanne's voice sounded harried beyond measure.

Maggie started to feel downright relieved. Louanne's problem was one Mac would have to handle right away. If he had been planning to start in on the subject of Judge Foley, he was going to have to put it off for now.

Mac looked a little grim. "Great. It's Saturday and I get to go chase down a plumber."

The answering machine began whirring and clicking, resetting itself to take more messages. They were in Mac's office upstairs, an open space that overlooked the main living area.

"So glamorous being in real estate." Feeling light-hearted now that she'd been let off the hook, Maggie leaned provocatively on the railing in front of the vaulting windows that extended from the floor below to well over their heads. "Living among the big trees, managing your own properties..."

Mac approached her. She continued to lean on the railing rather tauntingly. He put his hands on her shoulders and gazed at her gravely. "Never give me a bad time when you're standing here. I could get annoyed and toss you right over."

Maggie grinned at him. "I can see the headline in the Mountain Herald now: Local Land Baron Murders Girlfriend—Louanne McDuffy Still Waiting For A Plumber."

Mac laughed, tossing his head back and letting the sound ring off the ceiling. "You're developing a sense of humor, Maggie Durrant."

"And it's about time, too," she told him, her voice soft. Then she kissed him on the cleft in his chin. "You'd better get going."

"Come with me."

"No, I think I'll put my jeans on and get back to work."

His eyes probed hers. "Why do I feel like you're trying to get rid of me?"

"I have no idea." She was pleased at how unconcerned she sounded.

But then he cut right to the point. "You're going to have to deal with the subject of your grandfather sooner or later."

"Thank you, Doctor Manero," she told him tartly.

"I'm serious, Maggie."

"Fine. I've already dealt with it, as much as I intend to."

"He's the only family you have left."

She shook off his hands and moved around him. "He's nothing to me."

"That's not true, and you know it. Think of how you felt this morning. It was all you could do not to burst into tears. No one responds like that to someone who means nothing to them."

"He *hit* me. It hurt," she protested.

"I really don't believe he did that on purpose, Maggie. I think it's very difficult for him to be unstable on his feet. He looked terrified when he lost his balance. He struck out blindly, I'm sure of it."

"I realize that," Maggie said. And she did, at least in the logical part of her mind. "And I don't want to discuss it further. Not now."

"When?"

"Sometime. I don't know. But not today. I need more time." She looked at him levelly. "It *is* my problem, Mac. It's my right to decide when to deal with it."

Mac's face took on a resigned expression. "Well, at least you're admitting there's a problem." He tipped his head, and she felt that he wanted to say more. But all he said was, "I want you to really think about trying to make it up with him before you leave Brandy City. Promise me."

Before you leave Brandy City... Maggie quickly looked down at the floor. There it was again. Just like last night, when he mentioned how much he liked being single, he was reminding her that there was nothing permanent about what they shared.

But that's all right, Maggie told herself firmly. *That's neither more nor less than what we agreed.*

She looked up and gave him a smile. "Yes, Mac," she said. "I promise. I'll really think about it."

"Good," he said, leaving the railing and coming to her, taking her face in his hands and bestowing a sweet kiss on her lips. Then he left her to rescue Louanne McDuffy from the flood at her cabin.

Maggie watched him go, trying her best not to feel sad. She had known going in that what they shared would not last. It was fleeting, like the wild bleeding hearts and columbines that covered the hillsides in early summer and passed away before the turning of the leaves.

Like the wildflowers, Maggie thought. Gone too soon, but so achingly beautiful while they last.

Nine

During the long, hot days of the following week, Maggie finished packing up the contents of her mother's house.

She kept very little of what she found there: a hair ribbon of her mother's, her father's harmonica, an unfinished letter from Bryan that began,

Dear Maggs,
I have something I need to tell you, and I've been meaning to call you and say so. But then I don't know how you'll take it, and I think maybe I'll just write instead.

Then he'd written, *It's about the house,* and crossed it out.

Then, *I know how much Mama's house meant to you, even though you never liked to let on.* Then he'd put a line through that.

He'd made one more attempt. *There's a man named Mac Manero who's building a house across the creek and he offered*

The letter had ended there, on an unfinished sentence.

Maggie found it during her final hours of packing, when she'd at last decided to confront the piles of papers on her mother's old desk. She'd stared at the letter for a long time. It had not made her sad, though her eyes had filled enough that she had to dash the moisture away when the back-sloping letters of Bryan's lazy hand blurred before her.

Bryan *had* understood how she felt about the house. And his keeping the sale of it from her had bothered him. He'd even sat himself down to write to her about it. That pleased Maggie greatly.

Maggie put the letter, with the few other personal treasures she'd saved, in a velvet-lined box that had once been her Grandmother Olivia's. Then she sorted the rest of the papers, found a few bills, which she set aside to pay, and threw the rest away.

She glanced at her watch. It was near three in the afternoon.

Maggie stood up. She stretched, sparing a glance around at the empty house. What hadn't been sold, given away or passed on to the Sluicer's Bar Community Club for the next bazaar had been hauled to the dump. There remained only her mother's now-cleared desk and matching chair. Maggie had offered those to Allison. Caleb would pick them up in the next day or two.

The huge job of cleaning out the old house was done. Maggie's time in Brandy City was coming to a close.

Maggie drew in a breath and forced her mind away from the thought of how soon she would be leaving. She wondered where Mac was. He'd driven up to look at a forty-acre ranch several miles above Brandy City early in the morning, announcing he'd be back by noon.

Actually she wasn't surprised that he was still gone. He'd been busy all week, and rarely home during the day. Unlike the week before, he'd found no time to work beside her. He hadn't even set foot in her mother's house since the Friday before.

At night she'd rarely spoken of her progress. Since she spent the days sorting and packing, she had no desire to spend her evenings talking about it. And Mac really hadn't asked how she was getting on.

She'd finished more quickly than expected. She imagined he'd be surprised to learn that the job was done.

Maggie rubbed at the small of her back, which had grown a little stiff from all the sitting that morning. Then she stood still and looked around again.

The house looked very empty. Maggie decided that it was time to get out of there.

She took the huge plastic bag of discarded papers and the velvet-lined box out to her car and then drove around to Mac's house. There she ate half a sandwich and changed into her new swimsuit, a bikini with huge bright flowers on the top and the skimpy bottom. Then, determined not to let the sadness that was tugging at the corners of her consciousness get a hold of her, Maggie grabbed a beach towel and fled to the cool comfort of the river.

Returning from a long lunch with the owner of the Shady Creek Ranch, Mac had almost driven right by the old house when he decided to stop and look for Maggie there. He backed up and parked his truck in the clearing.

He didn't see her car, but that didn't mean anything. She often used his trick of jumping the rocks in the creek to get back and forth.

Mac was excited about the land he'd seen. It lay in a tiny valley up Saddlehorn Road, forty beautiful acres of rolling green grass surrounded by towering pines. The owner wanted a high price for it, but Mac knew he could talk him down a little.

Mac planned to tear down the existing structures and build a new cabin, as well as a new barn and a corral where a horse or two might be stabled. It would be a perfect vacation retreat for the right buyer. A great place to take a family, where the kids could run free, get back to basics, learn a little about what really mattered in life.

It was the kind of place Mac himself used to dream about, during the bad years right after his family was killed. Then, such a place had seemed an impossible dream.

Actually the more he thought about it, he might just keep the ranch for himself. He could afford it. And when he *really* wanted to get away, he could go there, to the absolute silence and the beauty of the trees. He and Maggie might—

Mac drew his thoughts up short, shaking his head. He'd been doing that a lot lately, including Maggie in things he planned to do. He really had to stop that. She would be gone in a few weeks, back to Phoenix, as they'd agreed. Fantasizing about her being beside him in the future would only make the parting tougher.

What counted was now. In terms of other people, now was all a man could ever really count on. He thought of Maggie's brandy brown eyes, her welcoming smile and the sweet, firm curves of her tall strong body. He was going to make the most of now, he decided as he eagerly pushed through the squeaky old gate.

The doors, which she usually left open to catch the breezes when she was working in the house, were shut and locked. Mac had to use the spare key he kept tucked beneath the porch eaves.

When the old kitchen door creaked inward, Mac saw emptiness. He called her name into the emptiness.

"Maggie?"

No one answered. He stepped beyond the threshold, and his boots echoed hollowly on the worn linoleum as he moved down the long kitchen. He glanced in the bathroom; it was empty. He climbed to the top of the narrow stairs. Up there he found nothing but more worn linoleum, a family of yellow jackets and the faded curtains, which hadn't been worth taking down, blowing in the gentle wind that came in the open window.

Last of all he checked the downstairs bedroom, where she had cried out her loss and pain in his arms. The old metal-framed bed, the bulky bureau, the cane rocker were all gone. The closet was empty.

By God, he thought. She's finished. She's done it all. We haven't got weeks left—we haven't even got *days.* . . .

He should have realized that, of course. Or he *would* have realized it, but this past week he hadn't been helping her out as much. Tuesday, there had been the supervisors' meeting. Wednesday, he'd been up at the Veneration Hill house. Things had just kept popping up that needed attending to. He didn't know quite how it had happened, but somehow he'd lost track of her progress. Or perhaps he hadn't wanted to admit how fast she was finishing up, so he'd put her progress from his mind.

And now she was done.

Mac decided he had to get out of there. The old house was just too damned empty. He was out of it and behind the wheel of his truck in seconds flat.

Maggie wasn't at his house, either. The open, fluid space seemed almost as empty as the dim old house across the creek.

He found her work clothes thrown across the foot of the bed. He decided she'd probably gone down to the river for a swim. Quickly he changed into a pair of swim trunks. Then, slipping his feet into rubber thongs, he went to find her.

He took the low trail that began at the southwest corner of his property. It wound through thick-growing black-berry bushes and down to the river's edge. He hissed a curse when his bare ankle scraped a thorny branch that snaked across the overgrown path.

He caught sight of her at the bend in the river, where the water ran swiftly. It was the place right below where Woodman Creek emptied in. A part of his mind registered her bright towel, laid on a sun-cooked spur of sand nearby, and her tennis shoes, neatly placed beside the towel. But all his focus, his concentration, was on Maggie.

Her back was turned to him, smooth and supple, ending in the blindingly flowered bottom of the suit she'd bought the other day in Grass Valley.

"Mac, I'll just never wear something like this," she'd told him.

"Buy it," he'd said. "Or I will." Mac smiled at the memory. Now that he was looking at her, it was easy to smile.

Maggie moved gingerly over the pebbles in the shallows at the river's edge. He started to call to her, and then he heard her voice.

"Ouch," she complained, laughing as she stepped on something sharp. Mac froze where he was, enchanted.

The roar of the river sounded like a purr. Mac was sure that if the river could feel, it would be feeling great right about now as it waited for a beautiful woman to throw herself into its rolling embrace.

Maggie dipped at the knees and then shot out across the current. She laughed again, a pleasured laugh that spoke of heated skin stroked with liquid coolness. The river took her playfully, and she tumbled with it, not fighting to cross, but rolling and surface diving and rising again.

Her toes touched bottom as she reached the top of the short rapids that followed another bend in the river to a deeper pool lower down. She found her footing and stood, flipping her hair out and over, spraying drops in a jeweled fan to glisten and fall all around her.

Then she turned and forged up the shallows, hip deep, her hands spread in fans on the water's surface. The water cut back around her, lapping the sweet indentation of her navel, caressing her hipbones and the taut flesh over them. Droplets clung to the full rise of her breasts and trickled down her belly to find the river once again. Then, where she'd first entered the water, at the place where the creek tumbled in, she tumbled in herself.

Mac didn't count how many times she rode the water down, strode back up, began once more. He only saw woman and delight—in an innocently pagan game of pushing upstream, then slipping out and riding down in joyous surrender to the river's arms on a hot summer afternoon.

Somewhere far overhead, above the umbrella of oaks and evergreens, a bird of prey called warning. Within the ground cover, there were the scrabblings of smaller creatures, safe now from the hunter but stirred by the distant threat. A lizard, which had become brazen at Mac's stillness, shot across his foot and back into the brambles on the other side of the trail. Mac ignored all of this. He was transfixed by Maggie, amazed that this joyous, unrestrained creature was the same woman who had looked at the world with fearful wariness not two weeks ago.

She had changed, healed, become whole. Her mother's house was cleared out. There remained the decision about what to do with the gold mine, and perhaps, if he were extraordinarily convincing, to talk her into seeing her grandfather at least one time before she left Brandy City— and him—behind.

Mac drew a deep breath. It was for the best that she was leaving. He was becoming far too attached to her. And they wanted different things from life.

Maggie rose from the river. Water sheened off smooth flesh and colorful fabric. She picked her way over the rocks to the sandy spot where her towel lay and stretched out upon it, faceup to the molten sun.

Mac slipped off his thongs and moved then. The brambles stopped at a small bank that dropped to a ditch formed by runoff from the creek. He jumped lightly to a boulder in the center of the ditch, balanced effortlessly there for a heartbeat and then swung his other foot to solid ground.

He hesitated where the shadows of the trees ended, several yards from where she lay in blinding brightness. She remained unaware of him, the sleek crown of her head pointed in his direction. Her soft mouth was slightly parted.

Her breasts rose and fell steadily, jeweled by the water droplets that still clung to her, evaporating now with the sun's burning kiss. She brought up an arm to further shield her closed eyes. She sighed and bent one leg at the knee, digging her toes into the hot, dry sand below her towel.

Something in Mac's chest expanded, a sweet longing that almost equaled pain. Soon enough she would be lost to him. But he would damned well enjoy her for as long as she was here.

Mac dropped his thongs beneath the trees and went out into the sun. He walked down to her feet and stood there.

"Maggie."

Maggie sighed and peeked at him from beneath the shadow of her arm.

"Mac." Her voice was lazy, as if she'd almost fallen asleep. "I wondered where you were."

"It took a little more time than I thought it would," he said. "You should see it, Maggie. It's called Shady Creek Ranch. It's a beautiful place."

"Are you going to buy it?"

"I think so."

She kept looking at him from under her shading arm, continuing to reveal the sweet side-swell of her breast. An urgency rose up in him, and he forgot all about Shady Creek Ranch.

"Mac?" She said his name softly. Her voice could have been the wind in the trees, or the distant sound of the river heard from his bedroom window deep in the night. "What is it?" She sat up.

"You're finished," he said. "At your mother's house."

"Yes." She leaned back on one hand and shielded her eyes again.

He dropped to his knees in the sand at her feet. The suddenness of the move surprised her. She drew her legs up a little.

"Mac?" she said again, unsure. "Are you all right?"

"Fine." He moved forward, and she leaned back, until he hovered above her, braced on his hands. "I missed you."

"Well, that's nice to hear." She sounded uncertain. He was making her nervous. It was obvious that she didn't know quite how to interpret him right then. He couldn't do much about that, since he himself didn't understand the conflicting emotions knocking around inside him.

"Mac," she tried again, "is there something—?"

He stopped her questions with his mouth. She tasted incredibly sweet, as she always did. He groaned a little, just at the wonder of tasting her lips.

"Mac?" she asked, pulling back a little, still wondering what was bothering him. But he simply lunged forward and kissed her harder.

Her mouth softened, and her lips parted. With no hesitation she twined her slim arms around his neck. She pulled him down so that he lay on top of her, taking his weight with a voluptuous sigh. She kissed him back just as hard as he kissed her.

The burning sun beat down on his back. Mac hardly noticed. The heat between himself and Maggie was all that he knew at that moment.

She moved, sighing, beneath him, her body sweet and strong and so willing. That was the miracle of Maggie Durrant. Once she had given herself the first time, she never held back.

She matched him, kiss for kiss, caress for caress. She laid herself bare for him; she offered everything.

His seeking hand, glorying in the feel of her, closed on the full swell of her breast. He felt her nipple, hard in the heart of his palm. She arched her back, moaning, giving him more.

More than he could take. More than he had asked for. More than he could handle. Everything. And then more.

"Oh, Mac," she breathed against his mouth. "I love you so…"

His heart stopped, hovering high up in his chest. And then it seemed to drop down to his toes.

He stopped kissing her. She opened her eyes. They looked at each other.

Her full mouth was bruised from his kisses. Emotions chased themselves across her face. First there was shock at the words that had fallen from her own lips. And then wonder as she realized that they were true. Then her eyes burned into his, seeking a response.

Mac didn't have a response.

Her eyes clouded over. Her gaze slid away.

"Maggie, I—"

"No! Don't say anything. Please." She pushed gently at his shoulders. He rolled away and sat up.

Maggie sat up, too. For a time neither spoke. They watched the river tumbling by.

"I think I'll go on back to the house," she announced at last.

"Maggie—"

"Stay here for a while," she said. "Give me some time."

Maggie gathered up her things and left him there. He sat for a long time, wondering how everything had gotten so damned turned around.

At last he rose and went to the river. He dived in and swam across and back numerous times, fighting the current all the way. After that he sat some more on the little beach, until the sun had given way to the shadows of the mountains above.

Then he got his thongs and walked back to his house.

Maggie was waiting for him in the living area, fully dressed, sitting on the couch. She smiled at him in a friendly but distant way when he came in from the screened porch.

"I've put my things in the car," she explained. "I think it's best if I go back to the motel."

Ten

Maggie stared at Mac, who stood across the pale pine floor. Her nerves were flayed raw.

Never in her life had she thought she'd tell Mac she loved him. She hadn't even consciously *known* that it was love until she'd heard herself cry it aloud back there on the beach.

But the word—such a short, simple word—changed everything. The word put a new, blindingly clear light on it all. There was no going back from the truth in that word. It was out and it was true and nothing between them was the same anymore.

Especially not after the way Mac had taken it, the way he'd gone stiff in her arms and looked down at her with distant, guarded eyes. That had cut her to the bone.

She didn't blame him, not really. He'd never been less than honest with her. She was hurt, but she wasn't angry. And, as Mac had taught her so well, the hurt would heal.

The best thing would be to get started on the healing. And that wasn't going to happen until she got away from the source of the hurt—Mac himself. Their time together would have been over in a day or two anyway; she was just speeding up the inevitable. She only wanted to say thank-you and goodbye and get out gracefully.

But Mac wasn't making it easy.

He stood there, massive and unmoving in his black swim trunks, his face expressionless. Normally Mac had such winning charm about him that it was easy to forget how tall he was, how primitive his features, how massive his chest and arms.

But now, without his smile, with his black eyes as flat and opaque as coal, he would have frightened a lesser woman than Maggie. Even she felt the first creeping of apprehension, like tiny cold fingers, up and down her spine.

He swore softly. "Go get your suitcase back in here. There's no reason for you to leave yet."

"No reason?" She looked at him disbelievingly and then repeated, *"No reason?"*

"None."

Maggie didn't quite know what to do. She hadn't expected him to stand there like some latter-day caveman and order her to stay. She'd thought he would be relieved, or at least admit the wisdom in her decision to go.

She stood up. "There is every reason. It's over, Mac. It was ending anyway, within a day or two. But what just happened at the river finished it for good."

"It's not finished," he said stubbornly. "We won't end it like this, with you running away."

Anger rose within Maggie. "I am not running away. I'm leaving early, that's all."

"You're running away."

"No! I am not!" She lashed out. "Who the hell do you think you are, anyway? Sitting up here in your gorgeous house, all alone on your hill, passing out judgments on other people's lives?"

"It's not a judgment, Maggie. It's..." He couldn't find the words.

Maggie realized she'd hit a nerve, and she just couldn't let it be. Perhaps she wasn't the only one who needed to face a few truths about herself. "It's what?" she demanded. "Easy? A nice substitute for really getting involved with someone? You take me in and you make love with me and you fix all my problems, and then you send me back to Phoenix, repaired. A whole woman at last. While you stay here and feel a little sad at what *might* have been, if only I could have learned to love Brandy City as you do."

"*You* were the one who established the terms," he reminded her, his voice as distant and detached as his expression had been when he'd heard her words of love.

"Right!" she cried. "Because with a man like you there are no other terms. You're funny and sexy and smart and good and you really care about other people—in moderation. But you don't want to get involved in any permanent kind of way. You found out when you were thirteen that the people you loved can *die* on you, and you're scared to get too close for fear fate might do it to you again."

"That is not true," he said, but the words had a hollow ring.

Maggie's heart twisted in her chest. She ached for him because she loved him, and she didn't want to hurt him. But somehow she couldn't stop the truth from finding its way out her mouth.

"Oh, come on, Mac," she insisted, "it *is* true. It's in everything about you." She gestured at the pale pine walls and vaulting ceilings. "It's in every beam and board of this beautiful house where there's no privacy, because you don't need for there to be privacy, because there's only you."

She went on, every bit as relentless as he had once been at exposing the truth. "And, whether you did it consciously or not, you only allowed yourself to get involved with me because you were sure I wouldn't be around long enough that you'd get too attached."

"That's ridiculous," he objected.

"Is it?"

"Completely." He crossed his arms over his chest. In spite of the power in his arms and the depth of his chest, the gesture was a defensive one.

Maggie knew she should stop prodding him, march straight past him to the door and out to her car. She should get in, drive away and never look back.

But then she realized she'd never be sure she should have left unless she knew the answer to one last question.

She said very calmly, "All right, then, Mac. I've given it a lot of thought, and I've realized that I love Brandy City every bit as much as you do. I've decided to stay, so now there's nothing to keep us apart...what do you say to that?"

He stared at her.

"Well?" she demanded.

"Maggie, I..."

"Is that all? Is that it?" She whirled around to grab up her purse from where she'd left it on the couch.

"Maggie—"

"Goodbye, Mac." She was out the door and behind the wheel of her car before she accepted the fact that he wasn't going to follow her.

Eleven

A half hour later Maggie sat on the edge of the bed in her room at the Rivervista Motel. She folded her hands in her lap and tried to think what to do next.

Her thoughts, however, wouldn't focus. Her mind kept darting every which way.

Though this was not the same room she'd had before, the layout was identical. Opposite her was the low dresser, with a mirror above, just like in the other room.

In that other room, she and Mac had stood before the dresser mirror together, both of them too tall to fit into the reflection. Moments later he had kissed her—a kiss so consuming that she had thought of flash fires, igniting from a single spark, setting the forest ablaze....

The pain of Mac's rejection rose up in her again, a rolling wave of hurt. She felt the stinging pressure behind her eyes, the lump in her throat.

"The hurt will heal," she murmured aloud, and looked away from the mirror that had brought to mind their first kiss. Her gaze fell on the window, which was open a crack. From beyond it came the chiding roar of the river below.

Maggie leapt from the bed and slammed the window shut.

She sat down in a chair. Then she stood up. She paced the room, feeling caged. She sat down again, at the little table in the corner.

Then she realized there was no way she could sleep in Brandy City that night. She never should have come here from Mac's. She should have turned southwest and kept driving until she reached Sacramento, and the airport and the next plane to Phoenix.

She stood up, intending to throw her suitcases back in the car and check out. Then it came to her; she needed to make some provisions for the Hard Luck Lady before she left town.

She thought of Caleb's offer and picked up the phone.

Allison answered. Her friend's gentle voice sent a fresh wave of pain washing over Maggie. She asked for Caleb, but Allison explained that he was still over at the town service station, which he owned with his younger brother, Vernon.

"He should be back soon, though. Come for dinner," Allison urged. "My special pot roast—you won't be sorry."

Maggie thanked her friend and promised to be right over. She left her car in the motel lot and walked to the Clay house, grateful to get out of the enclosed space of the motel room.

It turned out that Caleb was gone on a towing call, and Allison wasn't sure exactly when he'd return. They sat down to eat without him. Several times during the meal,

Maggie felt her friend's questioning eyes on her. Maggie smiled reassuringly at Allison and then looked away.

After the meal Maggie lingered, waiting for the absent Caleb, helping Allison and her daughters with the dishes. At last Caleb arrived.

He washed up and sat down to dinner, and he and Maggie discussed their business while he ate.

"I'm just not ready to let it go yet," Maggie said half-apologetically when they'd reached an agreement on the work he would do and how much she would pay him.

"The Lady still has promise, I really believe that," Caleb assured her. "Maybe someday—"

Maggie laughed. "Caleb Clay, you sound just like my father."

"Nothing wrong with having a dream," Caleb said.

Maggie had no urge to argue with him. She thanked him and rose to go. She turned to her friend, who was just hanging the dish towel on a rack.

"Allison, thank you so much for—"

Allison didn't let her finish. She grabbed Maggie firmly by the hand and led her out to the deck.

"Sit down here," she ordered.

"Allison, I really should—"

"Oh, stop it, Maggs. I'm not letting you run off without finding out what's going on. Where's Mac?"

"Allison, I . . ."

"Tell me what happened. That's what friends are for."

Maggie bit her lower lip and dragged in a deep breath. "There's not a lot to say. Really."

"Tell me."

Maggie looked at Allison for a moment, and then glanced out beyond the railing at the houses on the other side of the river. Finally she began, "Mac and I had an agreement, that's all. We agreed that we'd be together until I had wrapped up Bryan's business here. Now I'm done, and—'' Maggie's voice caught, and then she forced herself to finish ''—so are we.''

''Let me understand this,'' Allison said carefully. ''Mac Manero made an agreement with you to have an affair that would last until you left town.''

''When you put it that way, it sounds—''

Allison was beginning to get angry. ''That's outrageous. Of all the cold, callous . . .''

Maggie threw up a hand. ''Allison, it was my idea.''

''Excuse me?''

Maggie shook her head. ''I said, don't blame Mac. It was my idea. It just . . . backfired in my face, that's all.''

''How?''

Maggie started to feel trapped again, just as she had in the cramped motel room. ''I just can't go into it now. Please understand.'' Maggie stood. ''I really have to be going.''

Allison looked up at her. ''Where to, Maggs?'' she asked softly.

''I want to start back to Phoenix.''

''Tonight?''

''Yes, I—''

Allison shook her head. ''You can't run away from love, Maggs. Any more than you can run away from home. Both are always with you.'' She touched her breast. ''Right here, in your heart.''

Maggie stared at her friend, but what she saw—and heard—was Mac.

You're running away, he had accused this afternoon.

And that day at the mine he'd said, *Listen to yourself, you sound like a kid running away from home. . . .*

''Maggs, stay here.'' Allison was pleading. ''Stay with us. Just for tonight. Get some rest before you leave again.''

Maggie forced a smile. "You always make it sound like I still live here."

"That's because I think here is where you belong," Allison told her. "If you'd only listen to your heart."

I can't, right now—my heart is broken, Maggie thought. "I have to go," she said.

"Maggie—" Allison started, but then thought better. She stood up and opened her arms. Maggie moved into them briefly. "You call me, if you need me," Allison whispered fiercely in her ear.

"Thanks, pal," Maggie said, and pulled away.

Allison walked her through the house, where Maggie said her goodbyes to the family. Outside on the front porch Allison hugged her once more.

"Call me, I mean it—"

"I will...."

Maggie felt her friend's eyes on her back, unwavering in the deepening twilight, until the curve in the road took her out of Allison's sight.

She had crossed the bridge and was just about to turn to the steps of the motel when someone leaned on a horn in back of her. She turned to see Odetta Lafray behind the wheel of her truck.

Odetta had stopped in the middle of the road and was waving Maggie over. Maggie complied, rather than have Odetta shout whatever she planned to say for the whole world to hear.

Odetta didn't waste words. "Heard you checked back into the motel."

"I'm sure you did," Maggie replied. "I've been there for over three hours. If you hadn't heard by now, I'd be worried that something was wrong in this town."

"Don't get smart," Odetta advised. "What's going on?"

A small red sports car rolled up behind Odetta. The driver hit the horn several times in a series of short beeps.

"Odetta," Maggie said with a sigh. "This is hardly the place to discuss my private life."

"Fine," Odetta countered. "Let me just park this thing and we'll go to your—"

Maggie didn't let her finish. "No, Odetta. I don't want to talk about it."

"But you need to talk about it, honey." The sports car horn sounded some more, several angry yips, like an enraged Chihuahua. "Keep your pants on!" Odetta shouted, and then looked at Maggie again. Her hazel eyes that saw everything that happened in Brandy City were full of sympathetic concern.

"I'm leaving town tonight, Odetta," Maggie said.

"You're leaving Mac? Just like that?"

"Odetta, you know nothing about it."

"Because you won't tell me!"

"Odetta, I have to go—"

Before Maggie could turn, Odetta's skinny hand shot out the window and closed on Maggie's wrist. "Now, you wait one minute here. I'm gonna have my say, once and for all. Okay, you won't tell me what's happened, but I know you and Mac well enough to make a pretty good guess."

"Odetta—"

"I'm not finished. Where was I? Oh, yeah. I know you, Maggie Durrant. You decided early on that no man was going to get the best of you, and you had a valid reason for deciding that, I understand. But I'm telling you that there *are* good men, Maggie. Men who will stand beside a woman when it matters, who will be there through good times and bad, given half a chance. Mac Manero's that kind of man. But you got to learn that even good men need patience and understanding, just like us gals. And I hope

to God that you learn it before it's too late, I surely do."
With the same swiftness as it had shot out, Odetta's hand
retreated back in the window. "That's all," she said. "I'll
say no more."

Behind her the driver of the red sports car had begun
shouting louder than his yipping horn. Odetta gunned the
engine of her truck and popped the clutch. Then she re-
lented enough to add, "You take care, you hear?"

Maggie nodded. "I will...."

Odetta took off down the street, fast enough that the
impatient sports car was hard-pressed to keep up.

Maggie returned to the motel room and found that she
had somehow lost the energy to begin the trip back to
Phoenix. She sat on the bed and looked at her reflection in
the bureau mirror while Odetta's parting words played over
and over in her head.

At last she stood up, took her purse from the table and
went out into the night.

Twelve

<hr/>

Twenty minutes later Maggie parked her car in Mac's driveway. She got out quickly and marched up to the front door. She lifted her hand to knock and then heard the echo of wind chimes on the screen porch between the front deck and the back one.

Pulled by an instinct that knew no logical source, she moved toward the screen porch. She saw Mac immediately.

He stood inside the screen porch, bathed in the glow of the yellow porch light. He wore tan slacks and a black T-shirt, and he was rhythmically tapping the set of wind chimes shaped like long copper pipes against each other, so they sang out into the night without the aid of wind.

Maggie knocked on the frame of the screen door. He spun around quickly, like someone startled out of a trance.

He stared at her. "Maggie?" He sounded suspicious, as if he couldn't quite let himself believe it might really be her.

"May I come in?"

He stared at her some more. "I didn't hear you drive up," he said. "Because of the chimes, I suppose."

She smiled at him softly through the screen.

He spoke again. "Everything you said—all of it—was true." His voice was very deep and full of pain.

"I'd still like to come in," she said.

His brows drew together. "After knowing that?"

"Yes."

"Maggie—"

"Shh." She pulled back the screen door and stepped in among the chimes. She walked up to him, felt the tension in his body, the way he was holding himself back—and his need.

Slowly she raised a hand and laid it on his chest. His body clenched like a fist beneath her touch. "We need to talk," he said.

"Yes."

"But now that you're here, I don't want to talk."

"It's okay."

"I thought I understood myself," he muttered. "I don't. I know nothing of myself—"

"Shh," she ordered again, placing her fingers against his lips. With lightning speed, he caught her hand. He kissed her in the heart of her palm, just as he had done that night in her motel room. She gasped softly, her senses catching fire.

"I want you, *mi reina*," he whispered against her open hand. "Now. Tonight. If you stay, it won't be to talk."

"I understand," she heard herself answer, her voice husky and low with her own need.

He reached for her, fitting her body against his, tangling his hands in her hair and tipping her mouth up to his. He spoke against her parted lips. "What did you do to me, Maggie Durrant?"

"Shh," she said, and opened her mouth beneath his.

He swung her up against his chest as he kissed her, turning for the door that led inside. He went on kissing her as he carried her across the big living area, through the kitchen and the short hall, to his bedroom. He let her slide to the floor there, just long enough to remove every stitch of clothing she was wearing.

Then he picked her up again and laid her on the bed. His gaze licked over her, dark and hot, as he removed his own clothes. He came down on the bed with her, reaching for her, his hands claiming every inch of her, uttering beautiful words that she only half understood.

She opened herself completely for him when he moved above her. She took him within her with a long, eager moan. And she cried out her love for him shamelessly, again and again.

Then the fire between them swept all thought away. Maggie felt herself burn hotter and hotter, down to a white-hot ball of flame that suddenly opened like a flower of pure fire, its petals trailing sparks, setting the universe ablaze.

Slowly, some time later, Maggie came back to herself. Mac moved, taking his weight off of her, until they lay face-to-face. With incredible tenderness he stroked the sweat-dampened hair away from her cheeks.

"Maggie," he whispered, his breath still ragged from what had passed between them. "When you give, you give everything. I wasn't prepared for that. You took me off guard. I don't know if it's possible for me to..." His voice trailed off as he sought the right words.

She looked at his face and thought how she loved him, and knew she wasn't ready yet to hear what he might say when the words came to him.

"Shh," she instructed, rolling onto her back and pulling his dark head to rest against her breasts. "Later. Sleep now."

She was half-prepared for him to insist, but apparently he decided her way was the wiser one. Why ruin the beauty of what they had just shared with words that might mean they'd never share this again?

His head moved against her breasts until he found a comfortable position. He wrapped his arms tightly around her. And they slept.

Maggie woke at dawn with a feeling of great urgency. Gently she freed herself from Mac's sleeping embrace and put on her wrinkled clothes, all except her sandals, which she carried out to the kitchen with her so that the sound of them on the floor would not wake Mac.

She brewed a pot of coffee and sat at the peninsula counter, thinking. Then she heard Mac's bare feet on the floor of the hall.

He appeared, belting his robe and then going straight for the coffeepot. Maggie looked out the window above the sink, still lost in thought.

"What is it?" he asked her after a moment. She looked at him to find he was watching her. He took a sip from his steaming mug.

"I'm going to see my grandfather," she told him, setting down her mug.

"Now?"

She nodded. "And I'm not going to call or anything, so that if he turns me away he'll have to do it to my face."

"He won't turn you away, Maggie, I'm sure of it."

"Whatever. I'm still not going to call."

Mac set down his own cup. "Give me five minutes to throw on some clothes."

"No, Mac," she stated quietly. "I need to do this alone."

He leaned against the counter and tipped his head, studying her. Then he said, "Fine. I won't go in with you. I'll drive you to his door and wait in the car."

"Why?"

He had no reply ready.

"You're no more sure than I am of what kind of reception I'll get, are you?" she demanded.

"Damn it, Maggie." He threw up his hands. "How the hell do I know what will happen? I never claimed to be able to predict the future. I leave that to God and fortune-tellers. All I want is to be there for you if you need me."

How could she argue with that? Why in the world would she want to?

"Well?" he asked, his tone impatient.

She responded after a pause. "I'll go in by myself, agreed?"

"Agreed," he replied.

"Okay, then. Get dressed."

They were on their way to Brandy City ten minutes later. Both were quiet during the drive. Maggie found it difficult to speak, and Mac respected her need for silence right then.

By the time they crossed the bridge onto Mercantile Street and passed the Rivervista Motel, Maggie's heart felt like a jackhammer pounding on stone within her chest.

Mac parked his truck in an empty space in front of her grandfather's house. He switched off the engine.

He turned to her. "You're sure you don't want me to—"

She shook her head, not letting him finish. Then she got out of the car and turned to face the place where her grandfather lived.

The house waited, set back from the street, its sloping lawn bisected by a slate walk. A low wrought-iron fence separated the yard from the sidewalk. The iron gate opened at the touch of Maggie's hand, swinging inward on oiled hinges. Roses lined the walk, just as they had all those years ago when her father had died and she'd come here begging for help.

That was then, Maggie told herself staunchly. *This is now.*

Boldly she put her foot on the walk and forced her legs, one step at a time, to take her up the sloping yard to the wooden steps of the wide front porch. She mounted those steps quickly, before her nerve failed her. She marched right up to the door and lifted the lion's-head knocker.

She knocked sharply, four times.

Then she waited.

When she detected no movement within, she knocked again, even harder.

She waited. Nothing happened.

She glanced nervously out toward the street, where Mac sat in the truck. He leaned toward the passenger window and looked at her questioningly. She signaled him to stay in the car. Then she turned back to the house and forced the thought that Mac was watching all this from her mind.

Was her grandfather hiding in there, not even willing to come to the door and order her to go away to her face? Maggie inhaled an outraged breath. All the old hatreds washed over her once more.

The cruel, heartless old man was rejecting her again, just as he'd always done!

Maggie almost whirled to flee back down the walk. But then she drew herself up short.

If she ran away now, she would never know what might have happened. Perhaps, in reality Elijah was only sound asleep in bed.

But that didn't seem likely. While Maggie was growing up, Elijah Foley had been well-known in town as an early riser. He used to be there, waiting at the Gold Pan for Odetta to open up—until the daughter he disowned had started working there, of course.

Maggie had no idea, though, how early he got up now that he was so much older. Perhaps all the years of living alone after his retirement had brought changes in the habits of a lifetime.

Maggie knocked again, harder than the other two times. And then she forced herself to call out.

"Grandfather!"

The only answer was the uncertain song of a sparrow from a telephone wire above the street.

"Grandfather!" she called again, glancing furtively around, wondering if anyone in the houses on either side was witnessing the spectacle she made—Elijah Foley's disowned granddaughter, standing on his steps again after all these years, begging once more to be recognized.

She tried to look in the windows, but the heavy, dark curtains were drawn. Feeling desperate, she put her hand on the door handle. It turned without resistance.

The tall door swung inward. Even in Brandy City, most folks now locked their doors at night. But her grandfather, she realized, was of another age.

She turned quickly to signal Mac once more to remain in the truck. Then she grasped the door handle again.

"Grandfather?" Her voice hesitant now, she peeked around the door.

Beyond the threshold the musty front room was dim. Maggie had an impression of high ceilings, of hanging gas light fixtures that had been converted to electricity in a makeshift sort of way so that the wires could be seen creeping along the ceiling beneath layers of thick oil-based paint. The moss-green horsehair sofa and easy chair sported crocheted antimacassars across the back and on the arms.

"Grandfather?"

Maggie ventured into the house that all her life had been forbidden to her and those she loved. Opposite the front door, next to the arch that led to the wide formal dining room, lay a staircase of dark wood. Maggie stood at the foot of the stairs and called out. No answer came.

She went under the arch to the dining room, past all the heavy mahogany furniture and the glass-doored cabinet with her grandmother's fine china in it.

Beyond the dining room lay the huge, old-fashioned kitchen. Maggie stuck her head in there, calling her grandfather's name. He didn't reply.

A hall opened to the right of the dining room. The floor of the hall was carpeted in twining roses that reminded her of the old, dusty curtain that closed off her mother's bedroom in the house in Sluicer's Bar.

Maggie walked on the roses. The first door she came to swung inward to a blue bedroom with twin beds and lace curtains.

When I was a little girl, her mother had said once in a dreamy voice, *my room was blue....*

Maggie quickly retreated from the room. The door slightly down and across from the blue room was ajar. With a growing feeling of foreboding, Maggie approached it.

She had stopped calling her grandfather's name, because she had accepted the fact that, wherever he was, he couldn't hear her. With a cautious hand Maggie pushed open the door.

She saw more heavy furniture—a bureau with a mirror, a tall chest of drawers, a looming wardrobe where clothes might be hung. Leaning against the side of the wardrobe was her grandfather's cane.

The high four-poster bed projected out into the middle of the room. The crocheted counterpane of ivory lace was thrown back, revealing wrinkled white sheets and a slept-on pillow. It looked as if the lace counterpane was hooked on something on the far side of the bed.

Cautiously Maggie entered the room. She crept around the end of the bed, seeking with dread to know what lay on the far side and was pulling on the bedspread.

She found what she sought. Her grandfather lay unmoving, his body horribly contorted, on the oval braided rug. In one twisted fist he clutched the hem of ivory lace.

For an eternity of brief seconds, Maggie stood there, frozen to the spot. And then something inside of her seemed to break open, like a dam going.

"No!" she heard her own voice cry. "No, please! Not yet. Give us just a little time, please...."

She rushed to kneel at the old man's side, that part of herself that had lost everyone she loved prepared to feel the cold stiffness of death. She touched his gray, clenched hand.

It wasn't cold.

"Grandfather?" she whispered, hardly daring to believe.

She placed two fingers on his neck and felt the pulse that proved he lived.

Then he spoke slowly, in a hollow whisper, the words barely distinguishable. "Heard you—calling—tried to get up...Fell." Maggie bent down to hear and noticed that only the right side of his mouth seemed to be talking. She realized then that the deathlike rictus that had so terrified her was only on the left side of his body.

Maggie was no medical expert, but she was pretty sure he'd had some kind of a stroke.

"Stay here," she ordered softly. "Don't move."

As she leapt to her feet, she heard him murmur something that sounded like, "Don't worry." At that moment she began to actually believe that he might be all right.

"Maggie!" Mac was calling to her from the dining room. As she should have known, he hadn't been able to wait in the car too long after she disappeared into the house alone.

"Call emergency," she shouted as she ran to where he stood by the phone. "He's had some kind of stroke."

The next hour and a half was more or less a blur to Maggie. Fritz Laird was out of town, so Andrea Irving, a qualified EMT2, as she introduced herself, came instead. She arrived with a driver in the town ambulance within minutes of Mac's placing the call.

Andrea rapidly performed a few simple tests on Elijah, asking him to squeeze her hand and say a few words to her. Then she reported back to the hospital in Grass Valley, from which the orders came that she was to put the old man on oxygen and start a saline IV and then bring him in.

Patiently Andrea explained everything she was doing to Maggie and the old man. Maggie tried her best to absorb it all, but mostly she simply nodded and stuck by Elijah's side.

Andrea allowed her to ride in the ambulance for the hour-long drive to the hospital. Maggie sat in the corner, never taking her eyes from the old man, trying to stay out of the way so that Andrea could perform her job. Mac followed behind them in his truck.

In the emergency room, with Mac at her side, Maggie filled out a ream of papers while her grandfather was taken in for examination. Then the doctor came and spoke with her. He patiently explained that Elijah had experienced a rather severe TIA, or Transient Ischemic Attack. It was a kind of stroke, but one whose effects were temporary. TIAs, he went on to assure her, were in no way a precursor or symptom of more serious kinds of strokes. Elijah should have the full use of his left side again within days or weeks.

"We do want to keep him here for a few days to run tests, though," the doctor advised.

"Yes, of course," Maggie agreed immediately.

The doctor looked at her with doubting eyes. "Unfortunately that's not what your grandfather says."

"What do you mean?"

"Well," the doctor explained wryly, "the good news is that he already seems to be feeling much better. The bad news is that he's demanding, as best he can with his mouth half-paralyzed, to be released immediately."

"I'll talk to him," Maggie said.

"Right this way." The doctor looked extremely eager to turn this problem over to the nearest relative.

Once in the room the doctor left with the nurse and the aide who had been trying to keep Elijah in his bed.

"Good riddance!" The old man shouted after them with a half-paralyzed tongue as the hospital personnel fled without a backward glance.

"Grandfather?"

Elijah, sitting up with the aid of the adjustable bed, looked sulky, or at least half of him did. "Yes, Margaret." His *yes* seemed to be scraped from the back of his throat, and the *r*'s in Margaret were nonexistent. He glared at the far wall.

Maggie approached the bed. "Please look at me."

"Don't want to stay here." His *n*'s and *w*'s, like his *r*'s, weren't there.

"Look at me, Grandfather."

Stiffly the half of his neck that worked turned his head toward her.

"They want to run some tests, Grandfather. They need you to stay here for a few days. Please."

He said something that she couldn't make out. "I'm not some..." and the rest was a garble. Then she understood. *Guinea pig.* He was saying he wasn't a guinea pig.

Maggie's heart ached for him. An old man, alone, with no one. Determined to be tough, to stand his fate on his own. She knew that he himself was responsible for his aloneness, through his false pride and his inability to forgive; she knew it because the same fate could have been hers had she never come to grips with the demons of the past. She also knew that *she* held the key to make his last years on earth different than the barren, loveless time that loomed before him now.

"Stay while they run the tests," she said softly. And then she did what she'd never in her life thought she would do. She laid her young, strong hand on his gnarled one, on the left one, which was temporarily paralyzed.

His old, blue eyes widened. He gasped, a raspy sound. A single tear fell from one eye, down a deep groove in his wrinkled cheek and onto her hand that lay on top of his.

"Can you...forgive?" His voice seemed to come, clawing up, from deep in his chest.

"I think so," she whispered back.

With great effort he managed, "When your father died, I waited for your mother to come to me for help. Instead, you came. I . . . hurt you, took it out on you, because Julie didn't come. Can you . . . understand?"

"It still hurts," she admitted. "But I think, with time, that hurt will heal." He breathed deeply, and Maggie gave his hand a squeeze. Then she said, "Stay here. Take the tests. I'll visit you every day, and I'll be here to take you home."

"All—all right," he said with a jerking nod of his head.

Maggie left him soon after, when the nurse came back in.

Mac was there, reading a magazine, when she returned to the waiting room.

He stood up. "Will he stay?"

Maggie sighed. "Yes. He's agreed. I said I'd visit him every day. And come back to take him home."

"Is that a fate worse than death or something?" Mac asked, teasingly.

"No," Maggie smiled. "It isn't. Not one bit."

"Can we go, then?" he asked. She nodded.

He came forward and took her hand.

They began the hour-long return drive to Brandy City, along twisting Highway 49. The scenic highway climbed and then descended into a series of three canyons, crossing the Yuba on each canyon floor.

They were only five miles or so from Sluicer's Bar when Mac suddenly slowed the truck and turned off onto a dirt road that cut up the mountainside above the highway, into the pines and cedars.

"Mac, what in the world—?" Maggie began.

He cut her off with one quick look and then grudgingly pointed to a sign that announced: Skunk Creek Picnic

Area, ½ Mile. Fire Permit Required. No Overnight Camping.

They bumped over some pretty rough terrain until they reached the place where the rutted road ended at a barren, cleared space with an iron barbecue on a pole stand and a battered redwood picnic table.

Mac stopped the car, looked at the pitiful picnic spot and said, "This is no good." He reached for the key again.

Maggie put her hand on his arm. "Mac, what is it?"

"I want to say something," he said, more to himself than to her. "But not here . A whole forest full of beautiful places, and I choose . . . *Skunk Creek*."

"Wait," she said.

He paused just before he turned the key. "What?"

"This isn't Skunk Creek," she told him.

"What do you mean?"

She looked at him for a moment, feeling her love for him, accepting in her heart that it was time to hear what he had to say. "Come with me." She turned for the passenger door.

"Where?"

"Come on. You'll see." She slid down from the truck and headed off into the pines, trusting that he would follow her, not looking back.

About a hundred yards from the barren picnic ground, where the trees grew thick, she came to a ridge. She climbed down the bank, stumbling a little in her unsuitable shoes.

Skunk Creek, a crystalline stream that cut down the side of the mountain and ran under the highway below them, was as entrancing as she remembered from her girlhood.

The tall trees grew all around, creating shade and moist coolness. Moss of a vivid yellow-green and lilylike flowers covered the banks. When Maggie reached the edge, she paused to slip off her hobbling sandals. Then she jumped across in a single leap to the springy bed of moss on the other side. Mac was close behind.

He took her hand when he reached her. They walked together along the creek for a while, hearing the occasional squawk of a Steller's jay and the crunch of the pine needles beneath their feet.

Suddenly he stopped at a big boulder that looked perfect for sitting. Maggie perched on the boulder and waited. She'd found the place; now it was his move.

Mac leaned against a tree. "You're right. I didn't know Skunk Creek," he said after a moment. "It's beautiful, Maggie."

She smiled. "My father brought me here once. He knew every tree and boulder in this county."

"And so do you," he commented.

"I ought to. This is my home."

His dark eyes held hers. "Do you mean you're going to stay here?"

Maggie looked down at her bare feet. "Yes, Mac. I guess I started to know it yesterday, when I threw it in your face that I wasn't leaving. And then today, with my grandfather, I became sure. Odetta said she'll sell me the Gold Pan, and I'm going to take her up on it. I'm going to make it a miniature department store, knock out a few walls and—"

"Maggie?"

She looked up, pointing her chin high. "What?"

"Oh, Lord, Maggie..." He was shaking his head.

"Look," she told him bravely. "I know you're afraid, Mac. And like you said two weeks ago, it takes two to make a relationship work. I can be patient for a while. And eventually, if the idea of us together just ... isn't for you, well, then, I'll learn to accept—"

He covered the distance between them before she could go on. He brought her against him with one arm and took her chin with the other. "Listen to me, okay?"

She swallowed. "Yes. All right. What?"

"I'm scared to death," he said.

"I know, that's what I said—"

"But, sweet God, I love you."

"Huh?"

"I love you. Everything you said was true. I didn't know I was hiding from love until you showed me. And even then, it took me some time to admit the lies I'd been telling myself for years and years. But now I do know they were lies, so there's no going back."

Maggie stared at him, her heart seeming to expand in her chest with unbearable joy.

"But are you sure, about staying here?" he asked, his eyes probing.

"Yes."

He smiled then. "I *will* try Phoenix for a while, if that's what you want."

"I told you what I want, Mac Manero. I want to come home to Brandy City. And I want you."

His lips hovered a breath away from hers. *"¿Para siempre, mi reina?"*

"Yes," she said without hesitation. "For always." She tried to kiss him.

He held back. "We'll get married, have kids, get a station wagon, all of that?"

"Yes, Mac."

"I want you to see the ranch," he said, his breath warming her face. "Shady Creek Ranch. We'll take the kids there, sometimes. They'll love it. We'll have a barn and corral for horses, and they'll learn to ride— Oh, and I need to show you the house on Veneration Hill. It might be better than my house now. Better for a family, you know—"

"Mac?"

"What?"

"Shut up and kiss me."

He looked at her, his black eyes full of wonder. "Lord, I love you," he said.

"Prove it."

Maggie thought, as he kissed her, that she'd finally found the treasure that had eluded her father and brother for all those years. She had riches beyond measure. Love cradled her in strong arms, and she knew the place where she belonged.

* * * * *

Bestselling author **NORA ROBERTS** captures all the romance, adventure, passion and excitement of Silhouette in a special miniseries.

THE CALHOUN WOMEN

Four charming, beautiful and fiercely independent sisters set out on a search for a missing family heirloom—an emerald necklace—and each finds something even more precious... passionate romance.

 *Silhouette Books*®

CALWOM-1

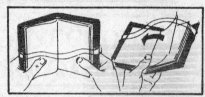

SILHOUETTE® Desire™

MAN OF THE MONTH

THE GOODBYE CHILD
ANN MAJOR

When passion and fate intertwine . . .

Rugged and ruthless oil trader Raoul Girouard was a man who would stop at nothing to protect gentle, sweet Evangeline Martin from danger. But could he protect this flame-haired beauty from himself?

Don't miss THE GOODBYE CHILD by Ann Major, Book Six in the *Children of Destiny* series, available in June at your favorite retail outlet.
